The Gambler

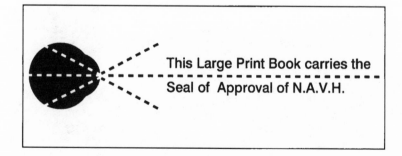

This Large Print Book carries the
Seal of Approval of N.A.V.H.

Max Brand®

The Gambler

Thorndike Press • Waterville, Maine

Copyright © 1924 by Street & Smith Publications, Inc.
Copyright © renewed 1952 by Dorothy Faust.

The name Max Brand® is trademarked with the U.S. Patent
and Trademark Office and cannot be used for any purpose
without written permission.

Published in 2003 by arrangement with
Golden West Literary Agency.

Thorndike Press® Large Print Western.

The tree indicium is a trademark of Thorndike Press.

The text of this Large Print edition is unabridged.
Other aspects of the book may vary from the original edition.

Set in 16 pt. Plantin by Al Chase.

Printed in the United States on permanent paper.

Library of Congress Cataloging-in-Publication Data

Brand, Max, 1892–1944
    The gambler / Max Brand.
      p. cm.
    ISBN 0-7862-5877-2 (lg. print : hc : alk. paper)
    1. Large type books.   I. Title.
PS3511.A87G35 2003
   813'.52—dc22   2003058171

The Gambler

As the Founder/CEO of NAVH, the only national health agency solely devoted to those who, although not totally blind, have an eye disease which could lead to serious visual impairment, I am pleased to recognize Thorndike Press* as one of the leading publishers in the large print field.

Founded in 1954 in San Francisco to prepare large print textbooks for partially seeing children, NAVH became the pioneer and standard setting agency in the preparation of large type.

Today, those publishers who meet our standards carry the prestigious "Seal of Approval" indicating high quality large print. We are delighted that Thorndike Press is one of the publishers whose titles meet these standards. We are also pleased to recognize the significant contribution Thorndike Press is making in this important and growing field.

Lorraine H. Marchi, L.H.D.
Founder/CEO
NAVH

* Thorndike Press encompasses the following imprints: Thorndike, Wheeler, Walker and Large Pr int Press.

CHAPTER 1

The mustang came over the hill with its head stretched low and long, while the little animal snaked it across the ground at the full scramble of its speed. It was a tired brute making a great effort at the end of a day of punishing work, but it at least did its best and the best of a running mustang is always astonishingly good. It works at close to top efficiency up to the stride that kills it.

So the mustang shot down the hillside with foam flying back and sticking to its working shoulders where the wet skin showed every grain and fluting of the muscles. The rider was a big man who looked even larger than the fact, because his horse was so very small; and the man acted like one pursued, turning his head time and again to the left to scan the point at which the road tipped up over the next hill before it dropped into the hollow.

At every glance he flogged the mustang with a sharper blow of the quirt. That little beast, exhausted and half blind, had still strength enough to shy to one side as a rabbit started up under its very feet and fled up the slope of the hill. The rider was nearly thrown from his seat by this side twist, but he clung with hands and spurred heels until he could right himself.

By that time, the horse had brought him to the edge of a dense thicket which rose over the road. Here he dismounted in haste. The horse which had seemed small enough even with the master in the saddle, now appeared hardly more than a great dog in size as the man loomed above it, dragging it forward into the shrubbery.

Then, leaving the horse with thrown reins, he worked his way forward through the brush until he was close to the side of the roadway. He had no sooner gained a position of advantage from which he could peer out in the road and the surrounding country, remaining concealed himself, then he uttered a faint exclamation of satisfaction. For he had seen a single rider just come over the crest of the hill to the west. He who lay in covert began to make busy preparations. It was stifling hot in the open where the wind stirred; but in the brush, where the branches were too thin to make any adequate shade, but where the foliage served to shut away every vestige of a breeze, he was in an oven. Moreover, every leaf and every stem in that thicket was gray with a powdering of dust which had been raised from the road in clouds by passing vehicles which had settled like the soft wings of moths upon the shrubs. And this dust, disturbed by the commotion he made in pressing forward, had been knocked into the air. It hung as thick as a fog in the brush, filling his nose, sifting between his bandanna and his neck, stinging his eyes and turning to rivulets of mud on his hot face.

He drew out a dirty blue handkerchief and mopped his eyes free of perspiration and dirt. After this, regardless of the focused sun which burned through his vest, through his shirt, and began to broil the flesh of his back, he pushed his rifle slowly ahead of him through the gap in the shrubbery until it commanded the road at his pleasure. Having done this, he gave his whole attention to the rider.

The latter had now passed the crown of the hill when the same rabbit which the first traveler had startled from a covert started up again and darted across the road. At this, though it did not shy, the fine black horse of the second man stopped and pricked its ears after the fugitive. Its master seemed in no hurry. He was willing enough, perhaps, to enjoy quietly the breeze out of the east which blew with pleasant coolness up the hillside and besides, from this hill he could look across a generous semicircle from the Santa Inez range on the north to that vast huddle of hills and peaks collectively called Comanche Mountain in the north and east, then over the narrow tawny ribbon of the Mirraquipa River streaking away to the southeast through a deep cañon, and so to the south where the bald-headed Digger range rolled away in rank on rank-like waves. Three oddly mated names to be grouped in one landscape! But the Spaniard, the Indian, and the American had all stamped something of themselves in this region. Just in the center of the arc stood San Pablo town with its white walls scattered on either side of Mirraquipa River.

The old Spanish town had suddenly started to grow again after a sleep of two centuries. Around those white walls there was an added girth like a thick rind around the white-skinned fruit of an orange. These were clustering frame shacks which had been hastily thrown up to accommodate newcomers, and the sunburned canvas of many tents blending with the unpainted pine huts. For a double good fortune had come upon San Pablo.

Far off among the tumbled crests of Comanche Mountain gold had been struck; within the same month silver was found in the Digger range, so that both yellow wealth and white tumbled into the little town in the same season. For a thousand necessities the miners sent to the city of San Pablo. All their wagon trains must roll through that universal halting place. And the wages and the raw gold and silver must be expended in San Pablo from Friday night to Monday morning. Already regular stages had been established to each of the two spreading mining camps. Even from this great distance the eye of the traveler could pierce through the crystal clarity of the mountain air and mark the dark streaks of the mule teams — ten and fourteen on a wagon, dragging up the opposite mountain slopes, followed by thin, trailing clouds of dust. And sometimes, though it seemed impossible, the broad wink of the sun along some animal's side, polished with perspiration, was visible as a tiny spark of light to him who sat in his saddle overlooking the scene.

He raised his glance from the town, from the roads, from the nearer brown mountains, from the distant blue peaks, to the pale blue heaven above, burning with the radiance of the sun. Even in the air there was stirring life; the buzzards drifted up, against the wind, in immense circles, wandering slowly toward focal points just above San Pablo. Seeing that, an odd thought came through the mind of the spectator that there was filthy corruption in San Pablo, and that these scavengers of the air were waiting for death.

He was not the man to hold a moral thought or a moral picture in mind for any length of time, however. Now he spoke to his horse, and that gallant stallion arched his neck a little and pricked his ears in response. As they went on down the hillside the rider drew out a handkerchief. It was not blue or red like the ordinary capacious bandanna of the range. It was purest white, newly laundered, and required to be shaken out of its folds before he could use it, after which he wiped his face clean, slowly, with scrupulous care, lifting his hat to dry the perspiration on his brow, running the cloth under his neckband, then whipping the dust off the sleeves of his linen coat and out of the wrinkles of his riding breeches and from the polished surface of his riding boots. For he sat in an English saddle, and his whole equipment was such as an English country squire might have chosen to don for very hot weather. His very horse was different, how different from the lump-headed, roach-backed mustang which had carried yonder fellow who lay hidden and sweltering in the dusty thicket. Such a horse as he of the linen riding coat bestrode would not have been out of place when the elect of Oxfordshire gather to hunt the first fox of the season. From its thin mane to its sparse tail, from its quivering nostrils to its black, hard hoofs, it was a thing of beauty. It walked as a cat walks, as lightly, as daintily. It galloped as a bird flies, with just so much delightful freedom and swiftness of stride.

Now it came down the hill flaunting the aristocratic little head as gayly as though there were not fifty hard miles behind it since that morning dawned. For it was thoroughbred in blood and bone!

Its rider was a thin-faced man something over thirty, though how far he had passed that mark it would have been hard to say. He gave an impression like his horse, of supple endurance and exquisite finish rather than sheer might. Plainly he had not been raised up under the blazing suns of the mountain desert. His face was pale, and that pallor was the more accentuated because both his eyebrows and his eyelashes were so exceedingly blond that they were almost

13

white — so very blond that his gray eyes seemed black by contrast. And the heat had only served to bring a slight flush into each thin cheek. Regarding his thin-lipped mouth, habitually a little compressed, and his rather high-arched nose, and his restless eyes, one hesitated to pronounce him more impatient by nature or more nerveless by constant and rigorous self-discipline.

He was apparently a man of contrasts, however. For if he had the face both of a conqueror and a tyrant, on the other hand, he rode with a woman's light rein and kept control of his mount, one might say, not so much by power of arm as by those infinitely subtle nothings which are telegraphed from the mind of a fine horseman, through the delicately sensitive tips of his fingers, along the reins as along nerves, and so to the brain and the soul of the horse.

He had come almost opposite to the shrubbery when his eyes caught a wink of the sun as small as one of those flashes from a far-off team toiling up the mountainside, but now infinitely nearer — at the very roadside, in fact! It was such a flash as it reflected from the smooth surface of a bit of shining quartz, say, or from well-kept steel. It was such a thing as makes an ordinary man merely turn his head, slowly; but the reflexes of this rider were like the reflexes of a wild animal which a whisper rouses from soundest sleep and which strikes before it sees, by the miracle of instinct.

With a touch of the spurs and a sway of the reins he made his horse leap sidewise half a dozen feet, and at the same instant his nervous hand whipped out a revolver and fired blindly in the direction of the thicket. There was answer more instant than an echo — the deep, clanging report of a rifle, and the muttering of the hidden marksman. The bullet whipped the hat cleanly from the head of the rider; before that hat fell halfway to the ground he had fired again, and this time at a definite target.

From the shrubbery arose a big man through a cloud of dust, knocked from the branches around him. He staggered straightforward to the road, blindly, his arms thrown out before him, and stumbling over a rock, pitched face downward into the liquid dust.

CHAPTER 2

The rider was instantly on the ground and, raising his ambusher out of the dirt, wiped his face first, then tore open his shirt. There was no need of a second glance. Here was a dead man, or at the least one presently to die.

The victim opened glassy eyes and looked curiously into the face of his conqueror, like a child wakening from a deep sleep. "What showed me to you, Corcoran?" he asked.

"Luck," said Corcoran. "What in the name of Heaven brought you here, Bristol? What had I done to you?"

"You cleaned me out last night in Eugene with some more of your luck. Handmade luck, that was, Corcoran!"

"You thought I cheated at the cards?"

"I knew it. Gimme a hand to stop this bleeding, will you? That slug —"

"Bristol, it's no use. You're a dead man, Harry Bristol."

The wounded man swayed in the arms which supported him; his eyes widened; his mouth gaped. Then: "That ain't true. It don't feel true. It's a lie, Corcoran. For Heaven's sake, gimme a chance. Gimme help! You ain't goin' to see me bleed to death like a —"

"Steady! Steady!" warned Corcoran. "You're nine-tenths spent already. I know something about wounds, my poor fellow, and I say that you're about done."

The other swallowed hard and raised a hand toward his throat with a grimace, so much pain did it cost him.

"I ain't quite forty," groaned Bristol. "What have I done to get this —"

"You've lived long enough," said the smaller man. "This cowardly trick of to-day is more than ought to be crowded into any one life."

"You ought to turn preacher, Corcoran, instead of gambler."

"When my wits grow dull, I may. But as long as my fingers remain supple I intend to live without labor, Bristol."

"You admit it, then!" cried Bristol. "You *was* crooked last night!"

"No," said Corcoran. "Not last night. To trim a lot of thick-headed fellows like you, Bristol, doesn't require cheating."

Bristol snarled like a hurt, angry dog. "Well," he said with a sudden resolution,

"I'm done. I feel it comin', now. But gimme a drink of water before you go! Gimme a drink of water, Corcoran."

"Certainly."

He placed Bristol against the bank at the roadside, carefully tipping his hat across his eyes to keep the fierceness of the sun out of it. Then he reached back for his canteen.

Both hands were busy with it when he saw the danger coming. Bristol had tugged the revolver from the holster at his side. His first shot sang past the temple of Corcoran; before he could fire again, Corcoran had kicked the weapon out of his hand.

"What a snake you are!" he said without passion.

The dying man regarded him wistfully. "That gun always pulled hard," he said. "If I'd shot at your right ear, though, I'd of blowed a hole in your forehead, Corcoran."

"Perhaps. Now, Bristol, here's your water."

The latter accepted the flask with suspicious eyes, first as though he suspected that the proffer would be taken back, and again frowning down as though he thought that the water might be poisoned. Finally, however, he drank, and drained the canteen dry.

He tossed it into the dust, which instantly swallowed it. But Corcoran, raising it and wiping the mouth of the canteen, said not a word in protest.

"Very well," said Corcoran. "Now tell me what I can do for you."

"You're a queer sort," breathed the other. "I dunno that I ever heard tell of your like, Corcoran."

His companion folded his arms. "You may make your own choice," said he in his quiet voice. "You may talk about me, if you wish, or you may tell me what I can do for you."

"What could you do for me? Gimme a passport to Heaven, Corcoran, or teach me a card trick to take to hell!"

"A fool," said Corcoran, "can never learn to gamble. As for a passport to Heaven, a winged angel couldn't carry you through the gate, Bristol. A cur who will shoot from ambush — why, man, when you get to hell in a few minutes even the devils will despise you!"

The bearded face of the dying man writhed into a sneer. "Preachin' ag'in," he said. "You *are* a rare one, Corcoran."

"For the last time," said the other, but without impatience in his voice, "will you tell me what commissions you to want me to execute for you?"

"Am I a fool to think that you'd keep a

promise to me? How could I ever know you'd live up to your promise?"

"If you recall what little you may know about me, you will realize that no one has ever accused me of breaking a promise."

"Tell me this straight. What makes you want to do something for me? Because you skinned me out of my money?"

"My dear fellow," began Corcoran, but he changed his mind and began again: "I shall not attempt to explain my motives. Let me tell you this, only; in the course of events, inevitably, I shall die as you are dying now, with another man or men standing over me."

"A smooth gent like you?" said Bristol, attempting a laugh and uttering a miserable choking sound only. "A gent like you? You'll get to eighty and give good advice to your grandchildren. That's the way things turn out in the world. Honest folks — they don't have no chance. Gents like you — well, the world is made for 'em."

"I tell you," said Corcoran as quietly as ever, "that a man can live in spite of a few enemies. But there is a limit. And I crossed the border line long ago. You might say that I have stolen the past five years of my life. Very well, when my time comes — when one man shoots me through the back or" —

he added proudly — "when a crowd dares to meet me face to face, I hope that they will at least do for me what I am willing to do for you."

"What's that?"

"For every twenty enemies, perhaps I have one friend. I shall wish to leave a small message, perhaps a small token, for each of them. Who are your friends? What message shall I take for you, Bristol?"

"Friends?" echoed the other. "The friends I have got won't more'n shrug their shoulders when they hear that I kicked out. I know 'em! Friends? I've had something to do besides waste time swappin' lies."

"No friends?" said Corcoran softly. "Well, then, there is some one of your family?"

"Nope. The old man and the old woman died a long time ago. My wife died a year after we got married. There ain't nobody."

"No friends? No family? Not a soul on earth who'll think of you after you're dead. Bristol? Dear God, man, think again!"

"There's my wife's boy," growled out Bristol. "Down in San Pablo, matter of fact. Unless the redheaded brat has moved along. He might remember me, for the sake of some of the lickin's I give him. You could find him and tell him I ain't goin' to have a chance to warm him up ag'in!" And he grinned broadly at Corcoran. A spasm crossed his face and he clutched at his breast.

"I'm about done," he said faintly.

"Very nearly," confirmed Corcoran.

"Look here," gasped out Bristol.

"Well?"

"About this heaven and hell stuff. A gent like you — you don't believe in it, partner?"

"Don't you?"

"I don't see nothin' very clear. Gimme your hand, will you?"

Corcoran kneeled in the dust and took the hand of the other in his thin, strong fingers.

"It's sort of dark," breathed Bristol, staring before him with great eyes. "About that other thing — I dunno what to think. Suppose that what the womanfolk and the kids believe was true. Like Santa Claus, Corcoran! Suppose that it was true — what a mighty lot I'd have to pay for! You ain't thinking that it's true, partner?"

He stared toward his companion out of blind eyes. His voice was a beggar's whine.

"If it were true," said Corcoran, "there's no reason why you should give up hope, Bristol. You know what the preachers say: their God is a God of mercy. Eh?"

"The sky pilots! But — a terrible lot of folks believe in 'em!"

"That's very true."

"Suppose — suppose — that one of them was here. Could he steer me right even now — after all I've done?"

"Would you want him to?"

"Think of goin' to sleep an' never wakin' up! Think of that! Think of bein' no more'n the empty ribs of a steer that the buzzards have picked! A man that could talk and think and remember things — how could we turn into dirt, Corcoran? How could we do that?"

"Perhaps we don't."

"If there was a church — man —"

"Bristol, you don't need a church. Repentance is the thing, they say."

"Corcoran, that's right — that's me! I repent. I don't want to be shut out in the dark — not with the hosses and the cows and the dogs, Corcoran! I want another chance — I want another chance! If there was a church and a sky pilot —"

"Steady, man! The Lord may be watching you all the time, for all you know. He may be listening to you."

"Corcoran, Corcoran! You're a smart man. What should I say to Him to hear? What should I say?" He clutched at his slayer, gasping out his words.

"I —" muttered Corcoran, "I don't know, Bristol."

"He'd want to hear me pray. Corcoran, tell me a prayer!"

"Why, Bristol, I think I know one — or most of it. Repeat it after me, if you wish."

"Not this way. They kneel in churches, Corcoran. For pity's sake, help me to kneel!"

So, sagging with weakness, Corcoran lifted the dying bulk to its knees, and the weight of Bristol swayed against him.

"Repeat it after me: Our Father, which art in Heaven —"

"Our Father," whispered the numb lips of Bristol, "which art in Heaven."

"Hallowed be Thy name."

"What does it mean, Corcoran? How can a name be hollowed?"

"There isn't time to tell you. Say the words. If there's a God, He knows your heart is in the things you say."

"Hallowed be Thy name!" breathed Bristol.

"Thy kingdom come; Thy will be done on earth as it is in Heaven."

"Thy kingdom come," gasped Bristol. "God a'mighty, give me one more chance. I ain't all skunk! Thy will be done on earth as it is —"

The heavy body slumped through the arms of Corcoran and lay on the roadside. Harry Bristol was gone. So Corcoran rose and dusted his knees, looking curiously down on the dead body.

"Very odd," said Corcoran to himself. "If I had to go through that again I might —"

He raised his head and watched a thin wisp of cloud as it hurried across the great arch of the sky.

CHAPTER 3

The sheriff of San Pablo county ordinarily kept his established office in the seat of the county government, that is to say, in the flourishing town of Eugene. Other sheriffs, in similar circumstances, would have wished that Eugene were even farther away from the battle front of crime which had recently been growing to prominence in San Pablo. But Mike Nolan had a childish way of taking his problems seriously. This one he considered with his usual gravity and, having pondered it for a week, he finally told his wife to pack the household furniture. Then he moved bag and baggage to San Pablo and on a day drove his team down the main street of the town surrounded by an ominous wave of silence.

San Pablo was not ready for him with a reception committee. To be blunt, San Pablo did not want him at all. It had other matters on its hands which required all of its time. Among others, for instance, it was very busy in extracting loose cash from the hands of those careless miners who wandered down from the mines in search of a good time with "trimmings." San Pablo had been supplying both pleasure and trimmings. A rich, steady stream of gold and silver was tumbling daily into the pockets of the townsmen, and they did not wish to be disturbed.

So, to begin with, they started to make trouble for the sheriff. On the first day they sent Ollie Haines to talk to Nolan. Ollie talked with all his customary eloquence, a Colt in either hand, but he had hardly a fair chance to express all that was on his mind. The sheriff spoke the first word, and thereafter for Ollie "the rest was silence."

San Pablo still was not discouraged, however. It looked about and called up its reserves. It found two men who were not only celebrated as warriors of knife and gun, but who had not the slightest conscience about making members in a mob attack. The two were none other than Chris Newsom, famous for cattle rustling and half a dozen murders, and Hank Lawrence, more famous for murders, but less known for thefts.

The two called upon the sheriff rather suddenly, while he was unsaddling his horse in the little shed which served as a stable for his "string" behind his shack. The sheriff received a slight wound on the upper left arm. Chris Newsom died on the spot; Hank Lawrence managed to crawl away into the night and died in the open field. They found him the next morning.

Since the town would not sponsor this cowardly attack by burying the miscreants or by paying the slightest attention to them, the sheriff put their bodies into his own buckboard. Then he hired three Mexicans to dig a grave. Most of San Pablo attended the ceremonies which were conducted without the aid of a minister. The sheriff made the funeral oration. It was brief but strangely eloquent in the opinion of San Pablo.

For the sheriff said: "Gents, there ain't no doubt that you can get me. A whole town is a lot stronger than any one man in it. But while you're gettin' me, I may be gettin' some of you. Besides, when you get rid of me, you've only got a worse problem on your hands. About the same time that you mob me, the governor'll be ordering out the troops and sendin' down a lot of handy boys from the State militia. Well, friends, you can do your thinkin' and take your pick. Throw in the dirt, boys."

And he went away while the Mexicans shoveled the earth into place over the rude coffins.

San Pablo retired to think, and having irrigated its brains with mighty moonshine whiskey, it decided that it was best to leave well enough alone, no matter how bad that "well enough" might be. There were no further attempts against the sheriff. He was allowed to come and go. When he went forth to make an arrest, he was not hindered so long as he did not make too many. And the sheriff saw to it that he did not make too many.

He wrote to the governor:

"The time ain't come to put things straight in San Pablo. San Pablo is having a bust. Right now it would take thirty killings to tame the boys down. And a lot of good men would be among them killings. In about a month San Pablo will begin to wear off its jags, and when its headache starts, I'll put on the irons and jerk things into order so dog-gone quick that the brains of some of these folks will start swimmin'. That's what I say and that's what I mean.

"But right now it strikes me that the best thing is to stand back and let 'em wear themselves down with friction. Here's two or three thousand gents all handy with their guns, mostly loaded with booze, and all ready to turn in at a lynching party where the sheriff will have to swing.

"In the meantime, they let me go my way. I don't arrest many, but I get the worst in the crowd. I get the most of the real killers. The small fry can go their own way. They shoot up each other and save the State a lot of money for rope and free board."

This was the opinion of the sheriff, and this was the opinion of the governor also. He was aware that the newspaper correspondents were happy to have such a primitive and delightful place as San Pablo to talk about. They would not begin to damn the official negligence of the State for a few more weeks.

Such was the state of affairs. The sheriff was every day a little more feared. And every day the people of the town came to see that if they disposed of him they were in reality only beginning a combat with a hundred-headed monster, the law. Besides, behind the sheriff the law-abiding citizens of San Pablo, though a distinct minority, made a solid bulwark. And even border ruffians had an instinct which tells them that their individual prowess with weapons is of no avail against the orderly movements of a large body of men willing to submit unquestioningly to leadership and authority, just as barbarians wonder at, despise, and dread disciplined troops.

It was at this time in his career that a stranger dropped into the office of Sheriff Mike Nolan.

He was a man of little more than the middle height, but so slender and withal so dignified in his demeanor that he made the most of his inches and appeared a tall man until another came beside him. He was a fellow with mild, pleasant gray eyes, and peculiarly pale eyebrows and lashes.

He was dressed in riding breeches, and he carried in his hand a riding crop. The sheriff looked upon him and marveled. But what he wondered at was not the appearance of the stranger but the fact that he could have entered the town of San Pablo and passed in safety through its noisy streets, full of drunken, rioting, reckless men. It seemed to the sheriff well worthy of wonder that such a thing could have been done. It seemed especially remarkable that the half-dozen villains who were lounging across the street from his office and house had not taken occasion to say a few leading remarks in the general direction of the newcomer. For even the sheriff, a man of faultless manners according to the Western code, felt his lip twitching.

However, the smile did not really develop. There was that in the stranger which

31

restrained him. The riding crop in his hand he carried as though it were a veritable scepter. His head was as high as though he owned all of San Pablo, and most particularly the house of the sheriff and all that was within it. In this fashion the stranger walked in upon Sheriff Mike Nolan.

Standing at the door, he removed the white silk handkerchief which was knotted about his collar. This he shook out, folded carefully, and then put away in a hip pocket. Next he removed his hat, with a second handkerchief dried his forehead, then flicked the dust from his clothes with a few deft and wide-embracing motions, and finally stepped through the door and presented himself to Nolan.

The sheriff, amazed, saw one who, it seemed, could not possibly have been spending hours under the blazing sun of the outdoors. Everything about him was jauntily cool; and in his shimmering boots one might have seen to shave oneself. There was a crowning mystery. So soon as the stranger lifted his hat, his pale blond hair was revealed, neatly and exactly parted, neither rumpled by the long ride and the friction of the hat nor blackened with perspiration. Yet yonder at the hitching rack was the horse from which this odd fellow had dismounted, a horse caked with the red dust of Eugene and the gray dirt of all the intervening miles. The sheriff noted all of these things, which have taken so long to describe, in a single flickering glance and in the tenth part of a second. Then he pointed to a chair.

"I am Thomas Naseby Corcoran," said the stranger.

The sheriff harked far back in his memory. Somewhere he had heard that name. It loomed half lost on the horizon of his mind. Mountain or cloud, he could not tell. In the meantime he noted with much surprise that this enunciation of a middle name did not seem offensive. And the sheriff decided that there was no other man west of the Mississippi who could have introduced himself with three names and seven syllables without being instantly laughed out of countenance. However, he also decided that none could ever address this man as "Tom" Corcoran. One could not even think of him as Thomas Corcoran. One needed the entire title to roll across the tongue, slowly, with dignity: "Thomas Naseby Corcoran!"

"My name is Mike Nolan," said the sheriff, and stretched forth his hand.

He let his hand drop with a sudden jerk, and his jaw thrust out. After all, the sheriff

33

was an Irishman, and now his blood boiled. For the stranger had not made a movement to take the hand of Nolan.

"Before we become friendly," said Corcoran, "I think you had better learn a few things about me, sheriff. For instance, you may wish to know about my business."

"You can keep your business to yourself!" said the sheriff hotly. "I ain't askin' no questions of you!"

"My business," said Corcoran, "is gambling."

At this, the sheriff opened his small, pale-blue eyes, set somewhat close together, like the eyes of a bull terrier. It did not fit in with his first conception of the newcomer. He would have staked a good deal of money that the other was at the least one of the new mine owners — perhaps one of those Easterners who had already bought up such large shares of the claims on Comanche Mountain. Now he nodded at Corcoran, somewhat at sea because of the foolish error which he had made and still angry because of the first impulse, though he was beginning to see why Corcoran had acted in this fashion.

"A straight gambler, I guess," said the sheriff, masking a sneer.

"I believe," said Corcoran, "that I am the

34

crookedest gambler living — when I am playing with crooks. I believe that I am as straight as any when playing with honest men. However," he added, while he met the sheriff's gaze with a level glance, "I thought I'd drop in here and get acquainted with you before I opened up in San Pablo."

CHAPTER 4

The sheriff was both amazed and amused. "This is something new," he confessed. "Dog-goned if I ever seen anybody go about his work the way you're doin'. Maybe you want me to go in partnership with you, Thomas Naseby Corcoran?"

"If you did," said the surprising Corcoran, "we'd both be rich in six months."

"Ah?" said the sheriff.

"Because," said Corcoran, "you have the reputation of an honest man and I have the brains of a crook. Mix the two together and you have something which is very close to the philosopher's stone."

"What the devil is that kind of a stone?" asked the sheriff.

"I beg your pardon," said Corcoran. "I mean that if we worked together, we could turn rocks into gold. But let that go. I'm not idiot enough to try to buy you, sheriff."

The sheriff grew warm with this delicate flattery. It is one thing to have one's honesty admired by other honest men. It is quite a different matter to find that even thieves believe in one's virtue. The sheriff's heart expanded. He had to bite his lip to keep from smiling.

"Well, Corcoran," he said more gently, "you're a queer sort. But you seem sort of square about it. You've come to work San Pablo, have you?"

"That's my main idea."

"Well," said the sheriff, "why d'you come to me?"

"Because," said Corcoran, "I'm a pretty lucky fellow with the cards. D'you see? And before I've been here very long, I suppose that you'll begin to hear reports about me. They'll call me a good many kinds of a cheat. But, Sheriff, when those reports come to you, I want you to think twice and give me the benefit of the doubt."

The sheriff studied him for another moment. Then he removed his spurred heels from the scarred top of his desk and brought them with a bang to the floor while he rocked forward in his chair.

"Tell me one thing, Corcoran. Are you prepared to fight your way among tough fellows?"

"I don't know what you mean, sheriff."

"Why, man, I mean simply this. You may

37

have been gambling peaceful places before this, and you may have run into no danger. But in San Pablo you'll find a crew of very hardy gents, Corcoran. They don't think nothin' of goin' for their guns. Colts do more talkin' in this town than folks do. The shootin' scrapes and the killin' would keep an addin' machine busy to keep track of them."

"Thanks," said Corcoran. "I'm glad to know all these things about the town." He looked at the sheriff so quietly and so innocently that Mike Nolan felt his heart expand again — this time with pity.

"Corcoran," he said, slapping a hand against his knee, "I got an idea that you're a good fellow."

"That's very kind of you, sheriff."

"And my advice to you is that you get out of San Pablo as fast as even a tired horse can carry you. Get out before you land in trouble!"

Corcoran frowned at the floor.

"Otherwise," said the sheriff sternly, "I give you about three hours of life in San Pablo."

"Why, what could they have against me, sheriff?"

"Nothin', most like, except the cut of your pants. They don't need to have nothin' agin' you. They'll shoot you because of the way you got your pockets full of handkerchiefs."

At this, Thomas Corcoran sighed and shook his head. "I suppose you are entirely right," he said. "But it seems too bad that the world should be full of such brutal people, sheriff."

"I'll have 'em in hand — with a little luck!" answered the honest sheriff. "I'm playin' my game, Corcoran. The skunks'll feel my hand on their shoulders one of these days. Don't you worry none about that, because it's going to happen. Just you get out of San Pablo and wait till times has quieted down."

"There is only one trouble."

"What's that?"

"I have a commission to execute in this town before I leave."

"Maybe I could do it for you, friend?"

"That's really kind of you," said Corcoran. "But you see, this is a thing which has been entrusted to me by a dying man."

"Ah?" murmured the sheriff. "Might I ask who?"

"I have to find the stepson of Harry Bristol."

"That red-headed young devil? You mean

Julia Kern's boy? You mean that hell-raisin' young thief an' liar and fightin' wild cat, Willie Kern?"

"I suppose," said Corcoran, smiling, "that's the boy I have to find."

"More like a son of Harry Bristol than a stepson. Dog-gone me if he don't take after the old devil himself. I never see such a boy! It'll be the warmin' of the whole country, what that kid'll do when he grows up."

"Maybe," said Corcoran, "he'll straighten up when he gets older."

"Him?" snorted the sheriff. "There ain't nothing in him to get better. There ain't the beginnin' of no good in him. He'd skin a cat alive for the sake of hearin' it yowl. He'd beat another kid to death for the sake of the fun of hearin' him beg for mercy. Darned if he ain't just like a young wolf."

"Ah?" said Corcoran. "I'm very interested in that breed. Besides, I have a message to the boy from his stepfather, as I said before."

"You mean to say that Harry Bristol is dying?"

"Dead," said Corcoran.

The sheriff rolled a cigarette and lighted it meditatively.

"They all wind up the way that they start," he said. "Bristol was always headed

40

for the rocks. Finally he went bust on 'em. Bristol dead! How come? Get drunk and pick a fight?"

"No, he picked a fight when he was cold sober and laid in wait for a fellow who was traveling toward San Pablo."

"The skunk! Did his gun misfire?"

"The other fellow happened to see the wink of the sun on the rifle barrel. So he killed Harry Bristol."

"The devil. But Bristol, Corcoran, was a devil of a fine shot and a sure man at —"

"Of course," broke in Corcoran, "but even the best of 'em have their unlucky days. Can you tell me where to find young Kern?"

"That little devil? I dunno. You start out lookin' for trouble, and the first that you find — Red Willie will be at the center of things!"

Corcoran stood again in the doorway. "In the meantime," he said, "thank you a thousand times, sheriff."

"Wait one minute, Corcoran. Do you happen to know the name of the gent that saved the law all the trouble of a hangin' by killing Harry Bristol?"

"Yes," said Corcoran. "I did it."

And he was gone.

The sheriff sat for a time staring at the

doorway as though he still saw the form of a man outlined in it. A silence had come over San Pablo. Though the pause he could hear the rushing of the noisy little Mirraquipa, and his glance wandered vaguely upward toward the ragged heads of the Digger Mountains.

"Dog-gone me," said the sheriff at last. "If I didn't make a fool of myself!"

He issued from his office and stood under his veranda watching Corcoran disappear down the street on the black stallion which danced along with mincing steps as though at the head of a procession with a blaring band behind. The rider turned out of sight down the crooked street, and the sheriff wandered across to the half dozen loungers in front of the Quinnel store. They greeted him with unenthusiastic nods, and yet their silence was a tribute.

"What's doing, boys?" asked the sheriff.

"Not much news," answered the nearest man. "Old Curtis had sold out up on Comanche Mountain."

"Maybe you seen the new gent ride into town?" asked the sheriff gently.

"We seen him," said two or three, speaking together.

The sheriff saw that there was something on their minds. "I'd of thought," he said, "that the boys would of thought he was a sort of a show?"

"Well, he was, in a way. But not the sort of a show that big Jeff Toomey thought."

The sheriff scanned their faces eagerly. Toomey was an old trouble maker in San Pablo. His bulky hands were constantly mixed in quarrels.

"What did Toomey do?" he asked at length.

"There was something about this new gent that seemed sort of queer to Toomey," said the oldest of the six, who now acted as the spokesman. "He was ridin' up the street. We could see it all pretty clear from here. He seen this gent in the funny clothes on the black hoss comin' down the street. And Big Jeff stopped him.

"Looked like he had a good deal to say. We could see him begin to point out things, about the clothes of the stranger. And the boys come out from Jessop's to watch and to listen. Maybe you could hear 'em laughin' clear over yonder in your office?"

"I heard something that might of been laughter," admitted the sheriff. "But my ears ain't what they used to be by a mile."

"Well, the stranger let Toomey talk for quite a spell before he answered back something that made big Toomey mad. We seen

Jeff haul off and make a swipe at the other gent, but the stranger he just ducked under Toomey's fist and give his hoss a touch with the spur. How he done it, I dunno. Seemed to twist Toomey around, get one hand in the small of Toomey's back, and the first thing we knowed, Toomey was out of the saddle. The stranger carried him over in front of Jessop's and dropped him under the shed. And Toomey lay where he dropped, writhin' and kickin' and grabbin' at his right shoulder. I guess his shoulder was busted. It was a dog-gone queer thing. Then the stranger come on down the street like nothin' had happened."

The sheriff drew a long, long breath. He could understand now the singular silence which had greeted Corcoran during his progress through the streets of the town.

CHAPTER 5

Ω

They were gathered about one large oak tree, a formidable crew. Some sat about the comfortable bulk of the trunk. Some sat in the low-looking boughs which shot out close to the ground. Some stood idly, or conversing in whispers. And an air of thought pervaded the whole assembly.

There were at least thirty boys in that congregation, Corcoran estimated, and they were of all colors. There were proud-featured, olive-skinned Spanish boys, holding themselves close, apart from the rest, conscious even at that age of their pure Castillian blood. There were young Mexican lads with deep brown complexions rubbed gray at the elbows and the palms of the hands and burned to rose in the plump center of the cheek. There were one or two Negro children with white, flashing smiles. And the smallest quarter of all was composed of the true and inimitable American boy.

These last could be known by something wicked in the eye and reckless in the posture. Their faces were already marked with thought and deep-revolving schemes of deviltry had stamped them with a premature wisdom.

One and all — saving for the Spanish boys whose parents were probably ancient and rich landlords and kings of the range — this motley group was dressed in ragged trousers which sagged beneath the knees, bare brown legs and feet, and a shirt, usually cast off by some member of the family, perhaps a faded blue of which the sleeves were chopped off just below the armpit, the neckband hanging loosely around the withered little throats.

Corcoran brought his stallion to a halt and surveyed them calmly. It was a full five minutes before the clamor which he roused subsided. These had not seen the exploit at the expense of big Jeff Toomey through which he had introduced himself to the respect and to the good graces of the whole town of San Pablo. While their elders beheld that spectacle, these young Tartars were roving abroad in search of a treasure richer than gold, to wit: mischief! There was nothing to hold them in awe as they stared at the stranger, and in fact, they broke into a crowing chorus of laughter.

It broke like a wave. In an instant all hands were pointing, all voices were jeering. His hat, his coat, his saddle, his boots — there was nothing about him which did not seem to them worthy of mockery, and as they jeered at him, they danced to points of vantage, under the low-scooping limbs of the tree, ready to swing up among the branches in a trice if he attempted to ride them down.

But Corcoran merely waved his riding crop at them. Then he took forth a cigarette case, long, thin, made of purest yellow gold and covered with exquisite chasings. This he opened, selected a smoke with care, and lighted it amid a fresh chorus of hootings.

For these young bandits already "rolled their own." A tailor-made cigarette was to them a sign, somehow, of ridiculous weakness. And they yelled at Corcoran from the tops of their shrill voices. He regarded them with the same quiet smile and finally he waved to them again, and smiled.

They became silent. They had expected, according to their up-bringing to be charged and to be lashed with the whip. They would have expected to be noosed in the lariat and dragged down from the tree. This mild surrender was a staggering blow to them. So, after looking from one to the other, the laughter began to die away a little. And, seeing that the stranger neither cursed them nor threatened them, and seeing that he gave them back their taunts with nothing more than a smile, their attitude began to change.

There is nothing that a boy loves so much as a novelty, unless it be something to which he can look up with all his soul. To the dignity of Corcoran these wild youngsters could look up. There was nothing like it in San Pablo. It was new in their lives and wonderful also. For here was a man whom even clothes and a strange saddle and tailor-made cigarette could not make ridiculous.

Here Corcoran spoke for the first time. "I wonder," he said, "if one of you could give me a little information?"

"He talks like a dog-gone schoolteacher," said one.

"Shut up," said another. "Ain't he polite enough to please you?"

"Sure mister," said a third. "Let's hear what you want to know."

"I am looking for a boy whom I understand is in San Pablo."

Their silence grew tense.

"I have good news for him," went on Corcoran. "If you can help me to find him,

I'll be a thousand times obliged."

"What's his name?"

"Willie Kern."

A groan rolled through the ranks of the boys. One who was older than the majority of his companions now stepped forward. He was a large-limbed youth who now thrust a thumb under the transverse strap which crossed his shoulders and supported his trousers.

"Stranger," he said with dignity, "might be that you're kiddin' us along a little bit?"

"I don't know what you're driving at, my young friend," declared Corcoran frankly. "I ask for Willie Kern and you ask if I'm joking. Of course not. I really must find him."

"Look here," said the spokesman. "I ain't rich, but I'd pay a pocket knife that's got one good blade in it and a sling shot that's a beauty — I'd pay that much to the gent that'd tell me where Willie Kern is — that —" The rest of his remarks were drowned by a shrill murmuring among his confederates.

"You're hunting for him, too?" asked Corcoran.

"Am I? Dog-gone his hide, if I meet up with him alone, I'll skin him and leave him raw. That's about all."

"And the rest of you?"

They gave voice like a shrill pack of hounds. They all wanted to be blooded, it seemed, on the frame of Willie Kern.

"How long have you been hunting for him?" asked Corcoran.

"How long? Why, along about a year and a half, take it all together."

"A year and a half! But haven't you a chance to catch him at school?"

"Ain't we tried, mister? Ain't we tried *everything?* If we lay for him in the morning, he's the last one in and the teacher don't do nothin' to him because she says she knows why he has to come in late."

"What's your name?"

"Ralph Cromarty."

"My name is Corcoran. I'm glad to know you, Ralph."

"Might glad to know you, too, Mr. Corcoran."

"It seems that the teacher is on the side of Willie Kern, then?"

"I dunno how it is," observed Ralph Cromarty, taking off his cap and shaking his tousled head. "But pa, he says that women folks is always sure to take up for a gent that ain't got no good in him."

"Why, God bless them, I suppose that's true. But do you mean to tell me that you can't get at Willie during recesses?"

"He don't come out to play. He stays inside and talks sweet to Miss Murran."

"That's the teacher, of course?"

"Of course. He don't do nothin' but sit there and tell her lies. Which pa says that every woman is more interested in lies than in hearin' the truth."

"Your father seems to be a philosopher, Ralph. But after school — can't you catch him then?"

"You see, Mr. Corcoran, he's always the first away. He skins out the door or even pops out through the window. Miss Murran, she lets him do pretty nigh anything. She don't care about him, but she makes the rest of us toe the line and march out mighty slow and regular."

"But what about catching him after you're finally outside the school?"

Ralph Cromarty stared helplessly around him to find an object which would fit in with the picture which occupied his mind.

"Look yonder, Mr. Corcoran."

"I see a speck in the sky."

"That's a hawk, sir."

"What about it?"

"Could you catch that hawk?"

"Of course not."

"No more would you catch Willie Kern. My pa, he says that every sneak is a fast runner. Me, I don't aim to run much. I don't aim to *have* to run!"

"That's a very worthy idea," said Corcoran soberly. "But what has Willie Kern done to make you all hate him so?"

It was too much for Ralph Cromarty. Thrice he essayed speech and thrice the words tumbled up his throat so fast that they choked him and thrice his mind was flooded with his swift ideas. Finally he turned and threw out his arms to his companions, appealing to them for assistance.

"Fellows," he said, "this here gent wants to know what Willie has done to us!"

There was a deep and general shout of indignation.

"Come here, Tommy!" called Ralph Cromarty.

"Look here," he added, as a boy slightly smaller than himself came slowly forward, one eye contused and swollen and surrounded with purple paint. "Look here what he done to my kid brother!"

"Ah?" said Corcoran. "How did he do that?"

"Caught him alone and hit him when he wasn't lookin'. That's the way always that Willie Kerns fights. He ain't got no manhood in him, dog-gone him!"

"I should think that the sheriff would take

a hand," said Corcoran.

"My pa, he went to the sheriff. The sheriff he said: 'Tell 'em to go and get Willie for theirselves.' So that's what we started out to do. We'd been huntin' for him for about a year and a half, but when the sheriff he said that, my pa he said for us to all get together and start huntin' for him whenever we had a chance. We been doin' that for about the last month. But we ain't had no luck."

"You see," said Corcoran, "that you ought to scatter out more. How many would it take to lick Willie?"

"If he'd stand and make a fair fight of it, maybe any one of us could lick him, dog-gone him! But the way he works, there ain't hardly anybody here that ain't been hit by Willie. Except me," he added proudly. "I guess that he ain't quite up to tacklin' me even from behind!"

"Suppose, for the sake of safety, that you split the boys up into fives. That would make about six groups of you. Think how many more places you could search! And when you caught him, six would be as good as thirty. Am I right?"

"You are!" cried Ralph.

It was apparent that he was general over his army. He gathered the boys around him with a whoop and in another instant he was making his division of the forces. Among boys, every degree of talent is known. Mature men may have their doubts of themselves and their fellows. The banker may despise too much the blacksmith or he may too greatly respect him for unknown potentialities. But among boys there are no mysteries. One is fleet of foot, one is agile of brain, each has a definitely rated pugilistic prowess, and here and there stand forth a few colossi such as Ralph Cromarty, who was equally prodigious of both hand and brain.

Accordingly, he could name his lieutenants instantly, and with such skill that not a one of them could be questioned. Each was a worthy and a valiant leader. Each was worthy of obedience and received it. The general in chief assigned them various places for investigation. He himself would remain at a central post of observation, ready to receive their reports from time to time. And there was no better place than the broad, old oak where Corcoran had first found them.

"I'll give five dollars to the boy who spots him first," called Corcoran. "And five more to the gang that brings him in."

That princely offer was greeted with a cheer, and in a trice they had fled out of view.

CHAPTER 6

Corcoran now dismounted and took his place beside the general and the general's associate, a thick-necked, wide-shouldered boy with the strength of a young bull. But his narrow forehead revealed his weakness. He was simply a faithful dog, a worshiper of the shining greatness of Ralph Cromarty. His eyes were never off that eminent commander. The lightest wish of the great man was instantly foreseen and fulfilled so far as it lay in his power.

From the place which Cromarty selected, young "Bud" Saunders hastened to kick away the fallen twigs. He himself sat down near by, at such an angle that he could command a constant view of the features of Ralph.

After the debate they sat for a time in a pleasant quiet. The wind fanned their faces cool until the perspiration raised by the talk had been dried. Then it fanned them hot again. The spotted shade fell over them.

Now and again a leaf came whispering to the ground. And a squirrel chattered far up among the branches.

San Pablo lay near at hand and beneath them, its white walls shining in the slant sun of the late afternoon, and around the true city was the broad, raw band of shacks and tents; and beyond the town the wagons rumbled forth and rumbled back. One could cant an ear through the silence and hear the muttering of wheels over the bridge which spanned the Mirraquipa and joined the two halves of San Pablo.

"And when you get Willie?" asked Corcoran.

There was a long-drawn sigh. Such a breath is inhaled by the pilgrim who sees, at last, the fabled domes of Mecca rising in the blue of the evening.

"When we get him?"

"What will you do with him?"

"Mr. Corcoran, what *won't* we do to him? I've figgered out some of the things that *I'll* do. I dunno about the rest. I guess that they all got their own ideas."

"How about it, Bud?"

Bud lifted up his brutal young face and a grin wrinkled his very eyes until they were shut.

"I know what I'll do," he said slowly.

"Did he ever tackle you, Bud?"

"I was in swimmin', once," said Bud thoughtfully, shying a pebble at a distance twig and hitting it fairly in the center. "I was all alone down at the swimmin' hole. I'd dived. Before I could come up, I seen something white and shinin' slide into the water right over my head. Then a couple of hands grabbed me by the neck. Look how he had me! I was down. I didn't have no chance. I dog-goned near strangled. I fought and kicked, but he just held me tight and there wasn't nothin' that I could do. Pretty soon things got all black in front of me. Then this here gent that had grabbed me pulled me ashore and left me there tryin' to choke down some air and feelin' pretty sick."

"That was Willie Kern?"

"That was Willie," said the boy.

"If you didn't see him, how can you be sure?"

The two boys exchanged eloquent glances.

"That was Willie," said Ralph Cromarty. "It ain't so much what was done to Bud. It was the way he done it. Pretty near any other boy would of been afraid of killin' Bud by holding him under the water so long. But Willie, he always knows just how far he can go. I tell you, Mr. Corcoran, he's a bad 'un!"

"However," said Corcoran, "we'll soon have an end of your troubles with him. Now that there's a ten-dollar reward out for him, and now that we've divided our company up into half a dozen sections, we're sure to rout him out of his hiding place."

"Darn!" said Ralph Cromarty, as a small twig which had been loosened from the limb of the tree just above him dropped fairly down his neck.

Reaching one active hand as far down his back as he could stretch his arm, he voluntarily looked up. What he saw brought a look of horror and fear and bewilderment upon his face and Corcoran, flashing a glance up in the same direction beheld a ragged youngster hanging at full length of his arms directly above the captain of the boys. How he could have come here was indeed a mystery. In the quiet hour of the day it seemed impossible that any living thing could have moved down the trunk or along the branches of the big old tree without raising a sufficient disturbance to rouse their attention. Even the light-footed scampering of the tree squirrel made enough scratching on the bark to be heard by their sharp ears. Yet there was the boy, and he must have maneuvered his way down from near the top of the tree. A few instants before, that same branch had been occupied by members of the Cromarty gang. Now this catlike youth had occupied the position of advantage.

These reflections, of course, went through the mind of Corcoran like a flash of light. In the same brief glance he could take note, also, of the lithe young body, the wiry muscles which stood out in strings along the brown arms of the boy, a pair of brilliant blue eyes, a flaring shock of red hair — the color of flame — and an expression of wonderful malignancy on the face of the youngster.

There was only time for this impression in the split part of a second during which Corcoran could look up. Then the impending weight slipped its hands from the limb and dropped. Poor Ralph Cromarty had not time to stir. Like the prehensile feet and the agile rear limbs of an ape, so the feet and the legs of the assailant wound around the body of Ralph while the shock of that falling weight flattened the latter on the ground and knocked every vestige of breath out of his lungs. Above him, for an instant, squatted the red-headed monkey from the tree, one hard fist poised for a finishing blow, until he saw that his enemy was indeed helpless and hopeless beneath him.

Then he swerved to his feet to meet the rush of stalwart Buddie Saunders.

That young hero, stunned by this sudden apparition and the fall of his idol, had finally lurched to his feet and charged like a bull, his head down, his fists projecting past it like horns. Midway to his goal he struck the red-headed boy.

All that happened even the quick eye of Corcoran could not follow. He saw the new-comer leap into the air like a cat and land on Buddie with clinging legs and darting fists. He saw the two go to the ground and roll over and over. He caught glimpses of the face of Bud, horrified, struck with pain. They bounded to their feet again, but all the heart for an assault was gone from Bud Saunders. He fled with a wild yell streaming through the air behind him and leaving his beloved commander to fight the whole battle singlehanded.

Worthily did Ralph Cromarty stand up to his reputation on this day! He arose with the breath still more than half battered from his body, gasping, his eyes bewildered by shock. Nevertheless, having made out the form of his antagonist, he assumed a fighting attitude, set his jaw, and waited for the worst with the patient silence of a man.

But the red-headed terror had no apparent desire to finish the battle at a stroke. He danced before Ralph and struck him across the face with his open hand. The return blow was a wild and roundabout swing. Then the young warrior danced back again out of harm's way.

"Get your wind back ag'in, Ralph," he said. "I ain't aimin' to lick you when you ain't got a chance. When you're ready, say when. But now I got you alone, Cromarty, and dog-gone me if we ain't goin' to have it out."

Cromarty nodded. He leaned one hand again' the tree and with bowed head hung there panting for a long moment. During this interval, the young stranger folded his arms and waited, but his mind was not inactive. Corcoran could see those dashing blue eyes scan the ground as though sapping all of its inequalities, taking heed of every detail near by saving, apparently, of Corcoran himself. Of the grown man this little destroyer remained perfectly oblivious.

Now Ralph Cromarty stood forth again, drawing a last deep breath. They cast their defiance in the teeth of one another like another fleet-footed Achilles, and another large Hector, tamer of horses.

"Are you ready to take your lickin' now, Ralph?" asked he of the redhead, tucking up

61

the ragged sleeves which half masked his brown, strong arms.

"Son," said Ralph magnificently, "when I get through with you, I'm goin' to have you lookin' worse'n dog meat!"

He looked, in fact, as though it lay in his power to execute his threat. He was taller, broader, in every way heavier than his opponent, and his strength was seasoned by the advantage of a vital year or two in age. To balance against this, there was only the activity of the red-headed hero and the flame in his blue eye. It seemed to Corcoran that a single blow must crush the smaller boy. But this was before the action commenced.

"Start in," said the younger of the two. "I'm waitin' for the old windmill to start turnin'."

"You'll be hollering out of the other side of your mouth," said Cromarty, "before I'm done with you."

"You?" said he of the redhead and the dancing eyes. "The way I get exercise is beatin' up a couple like you every day before breakfast."

"You pug-nosed runt!" sneered Ralph.

"Son," said the other, "I'm gonna soak you on your own nose for that!"

And he did. The brown flash of his fist was as inescapable as a rifle bullet. It crunched against the nose of Cromarty and sent a red stream spouting over his mouth and chin. Cromarty smote in turn, so heartily that he closed his eyes with the effort. The redhead bobbed to one side; by a fraction of an inch that tremendous swing missed its target. Corcoran sat up to watch.

"Your kid brother," said the redhead, "I made a mistake on. I only done up one of his eyes. I'll fix both of yours, you lop-sided —"

Ralph Cromarty charged into two stinging fists, one upon either eye, and stepped back again, blinking, already half blind. He lurched forward once more. Again that unerring tattoo, the lithe brown arms whipping home as straight as a pitcher throws a baseball, and landing with a spat as the ball lands in the catcher's glove.

"Stand still and fight!" shouted Cromarty, charging through thin air heavily laden with jarring fists. "I'll give you a quarter if you'll stand still!"

"I'll *take* the quarter without askin'!" snarled the redhead, and leaped at his foe.

They turned into a blurred whirl of struggling young bodies. It lasted only half a minute. At the end of that time Ralph Cromarty, with a crimson-stained face, lay on his back on the ground and the imp sat on his chest with raised fist.

"D'you give up?" he asked.

"You be darned!" groaned Ralph.

The fist descended with a thud.

"D'you give up?"

"I'll kill you!" screamed poor Ralph impotently.

The fist poised ominously.

"Wait a moment, my friend!" said Corcoran.

The redhead turned to him. For the first time the blue eyes rested fixedly upon him.

"Are you dealin' this hand?" asked the conqueror.

"I think," said Corcoran, "that you've forgotten something."

"His left eye, maybe," answered the redhead thoughtfully.

"In my part of the country, they never hit a man who's down."

The boy flushed to the eyes; then he leaped to his feet.

"Cromarty," he cried, his eyes on fire, "if I ain't been fair with you, you can take a free wallop at me."

But Cromarty rose stumbling.

"I dunno," he said feebly. "I don't see you clear enough to hit you."

"Go tell the rest of 'em that you found me, then," said the victor. "You ain't only a start for me. I want to get warmed up to-day."

CHAPTER 7

Even an enemy may give obviously good advice. Poor Ralph Cromarty could do nothing but turn his head and stagger down the hill. His glory had departed from him. He was no longer the invincible. Perhaps, to-morrow, he would have to begin again in the ranks and fight his way back toward acknowledged leadership. Oh, life was bitter, indeed!

The conqueror turned on Corcoran. "Looks like you owe me ten dollars," he said.

"Ten dollars?"

"For seeing Willie Kern and then for bringin' him to you."

"You're Willie, of course?"

"I'm him."

Without a word Corcoran drew out two five-dollar bills and extended them toward the youngster, but Willie Kern turned the brightest crimson; his hand did not stir to take the money.

"Look here, mister," he said. "I only

asked for it because I thought you wouldn't give it to me."

"Why, son," said Corcoran, "it's yours."

Willie drew back a little, standing very straight. He was as fearless and wild, indeed as the very hawk to which young Cromarty had likened him.

"I ain't no beggar," he said. "I don't have to go around askin' for something for nothin'."

Corcoran knew when a point must not be pressed. He put up his money.

"Well, Willie," he said, "you've earned the money, and it's yours whenever you're willing to take it. And, between you and me, I understood that you have only yourself to depend upon. Does any one take care of you?"

"Me? I don't need no takin' care of."

He talked with his face half turned away so that he could keep a careful outlook over the countryside.

"You make your own way?" suggested Corcoran.

"Sure."

"How do you make money, then?"

"I work for chuck and a bunk, mostly," said the boy.

"And what do you do?"

"Pretty nigh anything. I could rope, if I

had a hoss. You bet I can swing a rope and daub it on, too! But they don't gimme no hoss to ride. They got some waddles around these here parts that'd make your head swim to watch 'em work. But they won't gimme a chance to show 'em what I can do. Mostly I got to milk cows and such like chores that ain't fit for nothin' but the womenfolk. I'm a boss woodchopper, though."

"You make enough to keep yourself and to go to school, eh?"

The boy flushed, as though revealing a secret shame. "A gent has got to have something to do with his time," he said. "Besides, that's Miss Murran. Dog-goned if she can't talk you into most anything!" He added sharply:

"Why'd you want to see me?"

"I have a message for you from Harry Bristol."

"Him!" snorted Willie. Rage and disgust clouded his face. "What you got to do with him?"

"He thought you'd be interested to know that he was a dead man when I left him."

The cloud disappeared from the face of the boy. "Dead!" he echoed. "Well, he was a hand with a buckin' bronc. He didn't pull no leather even on the wild uns. They'll have to shoot their outlaw hosses now that

Harry Bristol ain't around to break 'em in! How'd they corner him? How many did it take to kill him?"

"Only one."

"You don't say!" He shoved his hands deep into the pockets of his trousers and with his legs braced wide apart, he stood regarding his companion and wiggling his brown toes thoughtfully in the dirt.

"One man and a little luck beat Bristol," admitted Corcoran. "He thought you'd be glad to know that no more whippings were coming your way."

The boy flushed again. "That was when I was a kid," he said. "If he tried it now, he'd wish he'd set fire to his house before he tackled me!"

"I believe it," said Corcoran.

"Look here, Mr. Corcoran, who done that there shooting? Or was it knives?"

"A gun turned the trick. I was using the gun, Willie."

The boy blinked at him and then whistled softly. "I know," he said at last. "Talkin' soft and shootin' quick. I might of knowed that was your kind." He looked at Corcoran with new eyes. "How'd it happen?" he asked reverently.

"I saw the sun wink on his rifle through the brush."

"He was lyin' there waitin' to take you when you wasn't ready?"

"That was about it!"

"Think of him," said Willie Kern, "bein' once the husband of my mother. Well, sir, dog-goned if it don't make me sort of sick."

"Look yonder, Willie. Some of your friends are coming back to find you, but I don't see Ralph Cromarty among them."

"He's peppered," said the boy, "and he's salted, too. Inside of a week they'll be ten boys in town that can lick him easy. Up to to-day they wasn't nobody that had a chance with him. Gents are like that. One lickin' sort of takes the heart out of 'em. About the rest of 'em — well, I seen 'em comin' half a minute ago."

"You don't need to worry, partner. I'll keep them away from you."

"Huh!" grunted the boy. "I don't need no help."

"You won't let me give you a hand?"

"Thankin' you kindly, I'll ride my own hoss!"

"But they're making a circle to shut you in."

"I'll bust the circle in two then," said this dauntless fire-brand, surveying the scurrying groups with a calm eye.

In another moment the two flank parties,

running at full speed, had joined hands. The circle was complete, and now it began to shrink in on its center, which was the huge oak tree, standing solitary on the hilltop.

"What can you do?" asked Corcoran.

"Shimmy up the tree," said the boy, yawning with a rather overacted carelessness. "But they wouldn't play fair. They'd fire stones at me till they got me down. Only other thing is to run right through 'em."

"What will they do if they catch you?"

"More'n half kill me," decided Willie aloud. "That's the fun of it. I'd move on out of San Pablo, but I'd hate to miss seein' some of them black eyes!"

He chuckled softly to himself, and the light in his eyes were the light in the eyes of a cat when it stalks the canary, helpless in the cage.

"You won't let me give you a hand?"

"D'you aim to stay on in San Pablo, partner?"

"I don't know. I may."

"Then you better not be none too friendly to me. They won't give you no vote of thanks for it. I'm mighty glad to of met you, Mr. Corcoran. See you later."

He was off like a flash down the hillside, running not toward the thinnest part of the line which hurried in toward the tree, but aiming his descent straight at a dense group which compacted and stopped its advance in order to meet his charge. From every part of the circle came frantic shouts of encouragement bidding those in the line of the attack to stand fast, for succors were coming. In an instant the boys were in motion toward that vital spot. And as soon as they were in movement, gaps began to appear in the line.

The able tactics of Willie were most apparent then. Just before the movement when he seemed about to crash into the crouched, waiting mass of youngsters straight before him, he veered to the right sharply as a hawk veers when it beats against the wind with a wing tip pointed down to the earth. At one of the near-by gaps in the line he darted.

Three or four, with yells of alarm, threw themselves into his path. They were like stubble before the breath of the fire! One dived at Willie. He leaped into the air and doubled up like a jackknife closing, clearing the head of the tackler. His knotted body drove into a second foe. Both tumbled headlong, but Willie was up like a bounding rubber ball. Two more were just before him. His brown arms flashed in the sun; the two

71

staggered back, and Willie was through.

As he ran, his head was turned over his shoulder, and his shrill, taunting voice floated back up the hill to Corcoran. There was no need for the fugitive to use his best speed. He merely lounged along through the sunburned grass, for the "gang," after a feeble, futile lurch in his direction, gave up all hope of coming up with him. Instead, they picked up stones and clods of dirt and hurled them in his direction in the hope that they might cripple him with an accurately placed missile. To this annoyance Willie gave not even the small attention of a turned head. Neither did he increase his speed, but, giving his course a zigzag current, he soon dropped out of sight over the top of the next hill, leaving his would-be captors discouraged.

The fight and the pursuit was over and Corcoran, feeling as though he had witnessed a scene out of a new Odyssey, swung into the saddle on his black horse.

The boys stood about in confused groups, muttering to themselves, panting with the labor of their much running, with here and there a few shrill voices of the leaders pointing out what had been done amiss and accusing those at fault recklessly on every side.

"Will you ever get him, boys?" asked Corcoran, as he went by.

"You bet!" they shouted furiously.

"Ten dollars," said Corcoran, smiling, "to the first boy who gives him a black eye."

And he rode chuckling back toward San Pablo.

CHAPTER 8

It was the golden moment of the day when he reentered the streets of San Pablo. The sun was newly dropped behind the southern shoulder of Comanche Mountain, and all the western sky was aflood with a yellow furnace flare which piled up high and then ran away like water until it had girdled all the horizon with brilliant light, and the mountains rose vast and black within that circle. He passed a group of half a dozen strong-legged gold seekers who were tramping toward San Pablo. He only needed a glance to write them down correctly in his mind. The raw force of the sun had scorched their faces. Their cheeks were red, their noses were blistered, their marching song had once served for a drinking tune in a college party. They had come up here to see "life" during their vacation, and perhaps — who knows — to find wealth. But, whatever they found, they would be repaid for their long journey afoot.

Corcoran felt suddenly aged and gray

74

with time as he went past them into the town. He had not intended to remain long in the place. It was only at the most a single stage in his journey south and east, but now he began to change his mind. It might be that the reputation which he had made too soon for comfort in Eugene would soon follow after him like an overtaking wave and reach him immediately in San Pablo. But in the meantime, there might be a few pleasant days. And in San Pablo, even his repute might seem not too black among so many shadows.

Such thoughts as these made him realize that even the vast West could eventually become small. He went to the hotel and asked for a room.

"Full up!" said the contented proprietor.

"Look at the register again," said Corcoran, and shoved a yellow-backed bill across the counter.

The proprietor squinted at him over the edges of his glasses. Then he began to turn the leaves of his register.

"Why," said he with surprise, "dog-gone me if there ain' a bed after all. Right up in the —"

"Look again," said Corcoran, passing another bill across the counter. "See if that room isn't about to be emptied. I'm sure you can give me a room to myself."

The proprietor stared at him again. This was a time when a tent rented in San Pablo for more than a double room and bath in Manhattan's most luxurious hotels. A whole room! Corcoran could see the word "millionaire" forming in the eyes of the other.

"A whole room?" said the proprietor. "Well — maybe it can be arranged. Kind of steep though, mister!"

"I'll stand the charge," said Corcoran. "Send out a boy to take my horse to the stable."

"How'll the boy know the horse?"

"Tell him to take the finest horse he sees," said Corcoran, and strolled out and up the stairs behind the puffing proprietor.

He rather enjoyed an indulgence in overbearing manners from time to time. When the room was showed to him, nothing suited. It was not clean enough; the extra bed must be removed at once. Fresh water must be placed in the pitcher. The proprietor was bewildered.

"I've seen some gardens in the town," remarked Corcoran from the door. "Have some flowers placed in the room."

"Excuse me, Mr. Corcoran," said the proprietor. "For man an' wife the rates are double —"

He went out for a stroll through the town and found it all that he could have wished, and more. The rich old Spanish flavor was still strong in it. All was noise and stir, now, with the main street thronging with cowpunchers, prospectors, adventurers of a hundred kinds. They were hunting for gold all day; they were hunting for pleasure all night. But when Corcoran turned from this confusion onto the side streets, he found a wonderful quiet. The children played in the dust of the street; through the open doors he saw the hearth fires, glimmering over the hard-packed, clean-swept floors. He was five minutes away from the roaring gold-camp town. And here he was in the drowsy midst of old Mexico!

Little alleys wandered blindly through the dark except where a lantern glowed above a gate or a door. He passed others sauntering in the cool of the evening — señoritas under their white mantillas and black, old men and their wives strolling slowly — all with the faces turning up, now and again, to the beauty of the stars. Sometimes he passed the sound of water falling crisply on hidden lawns from revolving sprinklers. Sometimes the delicate and peppery fragrance of a rose garden blew to him. The very roar of the main street in the distance melted into the silence and made it seem more strong. It was infinitely soothing to Corcoran. He told himself what he had told himself many a time before: He must make his "stake" soon and retire from his stormy life. He had had enough of main currents; he must find the shallows and the quiet waters.

He went back to the hotel. The room was transformed, and on the table by the window a great mass of yellow bloom and red overflowed the edge of a brown earthenware bowl. He sat beside it, breathing its perfume, and looking through the open window down the street. The great gasoline lamp in front of the hotel cast a broad circle of light that included the front of the house across the street and made its white walls stare back at him. Into that circle, too, curled the dust stirred by wheels that rumbled up and down the main thoroughfare or tossed into the air by the hoofs of a galloping horse. And on the sidewalks a veritable metropolitan crowd hurried and scurried through the gray film of the dust.

They were all there, the faces he had seen so often; the chinless, talkative men; the pig-faced rooters after money; the then, restless fellows designed to follow rainbows for the pots of gold; the lounging, bold-eyed miscreants, who were here searching for trouble in the first place and gold in the second; the stern, square-jawed men of might who talked little and acted greatly; the complacent men who were never without their smile for good luck or bad.

Corcoran pored over them as over the pages of a fascinating book. He forgot the mild resolution of the side alleys; he was in the main street again. He was a hawk hovering over his prey. When should he stoop, and where?

He opened his folding portmanteau which could be carried so comfortably behind his saddle. It contained more necessities than an average man — or woman, even — could have compacted in the large proportions of a trunk. An actor doing one-night stands hither and yon across the face of the map might have sat down to study and learn from this master of condensation. An old campaigner who can all but furnish a house from his knapsack might have marveled over this completeness. There were not only necessities; there were luxuries also. One could learn from this example how to tuck a whole suit of clothes into a corner, and, having supplied all the material necessities in small compass, have room in so small a space to fit in writing paper, a gold-backed brush and comb, a razor case and strop, and even — a tiny manicuring set!

Who else in San Pablo paid heed to the grooming of finger nails? But, as Corcoran was fond as saying: "A thousand little things make up the man; one little thing gone wrong is a man spoiled." And he did more than coin a saying — he lived up to it.

It took him fifty minutes of hard work even though he moved at lightning speed. But at the end of that labor, he was contented. When he stood before the mirror brushing back his hair, he knew that all would be well with him that evening. Then, slipping on his coat, he selected a final touch — a little yellow rosebud which he fitted into his buttonhole.

He gave a final glance — what man can resist it? — at the shining toes of his shoes. Then, as all men will do, he shrugged back his shoulders and prepared to sally forth to be looked at and admired.

That was a main item in his life. He must be noticed. The instant he stepped into a room, if his strange thin face with the colorless hair and eyebrows, almost white, did not attract all eyes, there must be other things about him which would enforce attention. That rose, for instance, should be enough. If there were need for something more, perhaps eyes that traveled downward along his neatly pressed suit would be arrested by the light gray spats which he wore!

Spats in San Pablo! He smiled to himself. And when he stepped down into the lobby of the hotel among the unshaven, rough-voiced men, he had his reward. A silence and then a whisper passed before him. He had achieved his purpose. All eyes were upon him. Men, young and old, were grinning openly at him. There were sneers of contempt. There were gaping mouths of astonishment. It was what he wished.

He lingered a moment in the room and then walked toward the outer door, slowly. How difficult it is to walk easily when many eyes are upon one! How large the feet became — how awkwardly the hands hung! Up and down the length of Broadway, in all the scores of theaters, among all the hundreds of well-schooled actors and actresses, how many are there who walk easily onto a stage? How few, how very few can leave the stage with grace? Some stride, some scamper, some lounge, some bustle, some stamp, some glide — but how few are those who walk quietly, sure of themselves? The few are the real actors, the great ones. And Corcoran might have been on Broadway!

For he knew himself and his power, and

like an actor, he lingered in the center of the stage, filling the eye of his audience. He saw, about him, lips parting in an insulting remark, but another whisper, started somewhere in a corner, began and washed with a sudden ripple around the room. Smiles began to disappear. Sneering voices were checked in mid-utterance. What had happened?

Then, as he neared the outer door, he heard the answer, spoken more loudly: "That's the man who busted Jeff Toomey!"

Ah, well, how quickly the fame of a small action traveled before one! He hung an instant longer on the edge of the veranda and delayed so long that, just as he was stepping into the outer dimness of the night he heard another voice which said: "That's Corcoran, the crooked gambler!"

CHAPTER 9

He had heard that same tone before. It followed him around the world. Sometimes he escaped from it for a week, or even a month. Then he heard it again, a mere whisper, but with a wealth of suspicion and scorn in it, and deep hatred, also. For what does the law-abiding man hate as he hates a criminal too clever to be brought to trial?

So it was with Corcoran. They hated him because of the rumor which followed him about the earth, and they believed the rumor because of his pale, thin, cruel face, his steady voice, and the way his gray eyes had of looking back.

Ordinarily he relished the very intensity of their hatred. It was the spice of life to him. To be surrounded with malice was to be surrounded with pleasure, to Corcoran. He was walking constantly among swords, and he enjoyed every moment of it. But to-night it was different. For some reason that sudden blast of disgust and rage fell like a burden on his heart. And he found himself walking slowly, blindly down the wooden sidewalk, drawing deep breaths but unable to blow the poison from his mind.

He met Sheriff Mike Nolan at the corner. The worthy sheriff was lounging against a gate post chewing the stem of a short pipe, most of which had already been bitten away, so that the thickly curling mustaches of the man of the law seemed on the verge of dropping into the fuming bowl of the pipe at any moment and being consumed there. The sheriff seemed to be regarding the stars intently, the shivering stars in the cold black night which arched low over San Pablo.

A young Mexican stopped in front of the sheriff. He was very drunk, very noisy. Apparently he had won much money at the nearest gambling table, and he was intent on spending both the money and himself on a good time. Here was a harmless man, an easy prey.

What the youth said, Corcoran could not exactly make out, though he heard the sharp rattle of the voice clearly enough. He saw the result of the speech most clearly, however. The sheriff reached a hand toward the youngster. The latter drew back, and a knife gleamed in his fingers. Whereat the sheriff's hand turned into a fist and lurched suddenly forward. The young Mexican sat abruptly down upon the ground.

Corcoran looked to see the handcuffs snapped instantly upon his wrists, but instead, the strange sheriff actually raised the fellow from the ground and replaced the fallen hat upon his head.

Corcoran, as he came up, heard Nolan saying: "I know you, young feller, though I don't know your name. I know you, though. And I know that it's the booze talkin' in you louder than your real self. Well, my son, I ain't goin' to ride you none too hard. Maybe I'd better lock you up and let you get sober. No, I guess the best thing for you is to get sobered up your own way. Go right along, son. Raise hell. Spend your money as quick as you can. Buy some more of that there moonshine. But I'm askin' you just for one thing. Gimme a look at that knife of yours."

He picked it out of the sheath at the belt of the Mexican.

"This here," said the sheriff, "is a sort of jewelry that you hadn't ought to wear. Besides, when you get into an argument, you do a lot of sharp talkin' with it! Run along, boy; but if I catch you with a knife again around these here parts, I'll give you a tannin' that'll make you think that your daddy was right comin' down your trail."

"Sheriff Nolan," stammered the other, who had apparently recovered his wits when he got a clear look at the face of the man of the law, "I didn't know you. I'm sorry —"

"Run along," said the sheriff. "Boys will be boys, I guess. But that knife habit is dog-gone unhealthy."

The youth, looking as though he had just escaped from a lynching mob, skulked swiftly down the street.

"There," said Corcoran, "goes a fellow who will have quiet manners for half a week. I see that you are of the new school and believe in preventing crime rather than punishing it, sheriff."

Mike Nolan turned upon the newcomer with a grim chuckle. Certainly it was the first time in his life that such a tribute had been paid to him. When he saw the man who had addressed him, however, his chuckle ceased and he began to blink in wonder. For the main street of San Pablo was fairly well illumined with shafts of light which poured through open windows and through the open door. By that scattering radiance, the sheriff made out the natty attire of the stranger. And, finally, his glance settled with wonder upon the crowning touch of the gambler's costume.

This was a slender cane of the finest ebony, so polished that it hung from the hand of Corcoran like a glimmering streak.

"Ah," muttered the sheriff at last, fastening his gaze upon the face of the other and making out the glint of blond eyebrows above the dark eyes. "You're Corcoran?"

"That's right."

The sheriff stepped nearer. He raised his hand as though about to place it upon the shoulder of his companion, but checked the gesture. Perhaps he feared that his dusty hand would leave a mark upon the well-brushed coat.

"Corcoran," he said, "I'm after hearin' about you."

"I gather," said Corcoran, "that some of my friends have followed me to San Pablo. Have they been gossiping?"

"You might put it that way. They been talkin'."

"Well," said Corcoran lightly. "I hope they haven't flattered me too much. One's friends have a way about them, you know. Don't take everything for granted that you hear."

"Which a man might say they's talk *and* talk," said the sheriff. "But this was the kind that was hitched up pretty close to names and dates."

"You interest me more and more," said Corcoran.

"It interested *me* more and more the more I heard, which I ain't one that hangs around tryin' to peek through cracks or listen around corners to learn things."

"I believe that you are not," said Corcoran, bowing a little to give an added gravity to his compliment. "What are some of the names and dates you have learned about me, sheriff?"

"Most like," said the sheriff dryly, "they ain't no truth in what I've heard."

"However, we'll listen."

"Well," said the sheriff, folding his thick arms and looking his companion fairly between the eyes, "they's the case of a gent over in Butte City. That was three years back. He was a two-fisted fightin' fool — a regular hell raiser for fair. They still talk about him in Butte City. He was as wild as a crazy colt, and he was as dog-gone good natured as a girl that's fallen in love. That was the way Ches Oliphant was. Maybe you ain't heard that name, Corcoran?"

"It seems to me," said Corcoran, "that I've heard it. It has a vaguely familiar ring."

"Well," said the sheriff, "of course there wasn't much to your meeting with Ches. You and him met up and got to argufyin' up in Butte City. All you did was to kill Ches. Most like you ain't able to remember none of them little things so far back."

"Of course," said the gambler, "you are merely repeating gossip — not stuff which you believe yourself."

"Sure," said the sheriff. "I ain't no judge and jury. I can't arrest no man till he's got a warrant agin' him, neither. Well, they's other little stories. About a year after they say you done for Oliphant you was down in Phoenix. Arizona sure agreed with you. Sort of thawed you out after gettin' all chilled way up in Montana for so long. You got limbered up and got fired up on a minin' proposition — which the talkin' you done was pretty fine, but the trouble was that they wasn't a mite of a mine behind the talk. Not a mite! Lefty Guiness came and told you about it. He didn't live to tell nobody else what he suspected. Lefty was a sure-enough fightin' man. He was a hell cracker ridin' on a barrel of powder, Lefty was. But you killed Guiness and you stopped up all of that talk until you'd sold —"

"Sheriff," said the gambler, "that unfortunate matter of the Loftus mine was one in which I was myself given false information because it was thought that I could sell —"

"Sure," admitted the sheriff. "They

thought that you might be able to sell that same false information. Dog-gone me if they wasn't clever, them cold-blooded, hardhearted crooks that raked in a gent like you. Dog-gone if I don't believe that you've hardly had one good night's sleep since the time you left Phoenix."

The brow of the gambler was certainly a brow of marble. He met the fierce eye of the sheriff unperturbed and, tucking his slender stick under one arm, he produced and snapped open that long, thin, golden cigarette case. The sheriff refused a smoke with a snort and then watched, like a fascinated child, while Corcoran lighted a cigarette and restored the case to his pocket.

"Last year," said the sheriff, "the best gun fighter in Morriston was Hank Curry. Hank got into a gambling game with a gent that went by your name, Corcoran. Most like you forget what happened."

"I remember it very well," said Corcoran. "The idiot accused me of cheating. I was forced to call him a fool. Afterward I saw the body properly interred. I could do no more, could I, Sheriff Nolan?"

The sheriff grunted. "These here things that I've told you," he said, "is only a part of what I've been told. They's a lot more. But what I aim to say now is that no matter whether they're true or not, I got to whisper in your ear something you hadn't ought to forget, Corcoran."

"Whatever you say," said Corcoran, "I shall remember as if I had read it in a Bible."

The sheriff scowled again. "It's just this: Things is pretty rough here in San Pablo. I can't watch everything. But I keep an eye on the headliners. And if you ever have the bad luck to pull a gun on a gent in this here town, Corcoran, I'm comin' to get you, quick. They ain't goin' to be no questions asked. I'm comin' to get you and stick you behind the bars of the jail. That's short and easy to tuck away into your memory, I guess."

"Certainly," said Corcoran. "But, sheriff, I want you to remember that I am a man of peace. You understand me, of course?"

"Sure," grunted the sheriff, and turned on his heel.

As for Corcoran, he had hardly resumed his journey along the street when he made out a familiar figure just before him, bareheaded, with the light from every window he passed flaring upon flame-red hair. It was Willie Kern.

CHAPTER 10

The light-footed Willie was stealing along close to the fronts of the buildings, dipping in and out of shadowy doorways, sliding dexterously in among the crowd. Except for the occasional flash of light on his red hair, the gambler would have found it almost impossible to trail the youngster.

He discovered, very soon, that Willie was trailing some one else, just as he was trailing Willie. Whenever the distant figure paused, Willie paused also; when it advanced, he went forward. It was a young woman. The slender form and the quick step told Corcoran that much. It was a young woman with plenty of self-reliance. That was equally evident or else she would not have ventured alone among the ruffians who thronged the streets of San Pablo at night. And she was a person whose character must show in her face, since not one of the half-drunk fellows who reeled along the sidewalk dared to accost her. They let her pass, and she went through the noisy, dusty, shouting, wrangling crowd like a free spirit possessed of a charm. Tangles of men dissolved before her and gave her way. Hats were lifted and cheery words spoken; and she, waving back to them, went lightly on her way.

It struck Corcoran at once that this must be the only person in San Pablo who dared to sympathize with Willie Kern. This could be none other than Miss Kitty Murran herself. Corcoran redoubled his pace and came closer behind Willie.

The girl now turned from the main street into a darkened alley. Corcoran, following Willie in turn behind her, saw her, as he came into the mouth of the by street, pass on into the dim light of a small avenue beyond. Willie was now halfway between her and Corcoran, passing the light of an open door, when Corcoran saw something like a shadowy snake scoop into the air above the head of the boy and then settle swiftly upon him. He was jerked prostrate and at the same time a wild yell of triumph rang through the alleyway while a dozen small forms darted out at the prostrate victim.

Corcoran came up on the run. To his first command there was no reply. Many a pair of hands were busy trussing him; many a shrill young voice was pouring insults and taunts upon him; and Willie Kern, all the while, lay where he had fallen, seeing that resistance was in vain, looking grimly upon his captors.

The flexible ebony cane sang twice through the air and twice shouts of pain answered him. Then he stood over the victim.

"Ten to one is hardly fair, lads," said Corcoran.

They hung about him, glowering, trembling with savage eagerness, like so many half wild dogs from which a body had been dragged by a single wolf.

"It's the gambler! It's Corcoran!" shrilled one youth, still dancing with the cutting pain of Corcoran's stroke. "Let's grab him, fellers!"

They were quite capable of it. There were sinewy, athletic youngsters verging on fourteen years, faster than men in their motions, almost as strong of hand as any cowpuncher. Corcoran saw that his back was to the wall. He needed assistance and at his very feet lay, perhaps, the help which he wanted. He leaned and freed the boy with a few touches of his knife, and Willie leaped to his feet beside his rescuer.

"Start in, Buddie!" yelled one of his assailants. "You just start, and we'll foller you! We can clean up on both of 'em!"

"Sure," said Willie Kern. "Start something, Bud. You run away too dog-gone fast today for me to get a good chance at you. Start in, Bud! Ain't we waitin' for you?"

A murmur of rage broke from the throats of the pack. Willie turned to Corcoran.

"Shall I soak Bud?" he asked calmly.

"Let Bud alone," said Corcoran. "Walk behind me, Willie. Now, boys," he went on, twirling the cane in the air until it became a dim but solid disk of light, "if I have any trouble with you, I'll take the lot of you, skin you, and use the hides for a saddle. Stand away, sons!"

They gave way sullenly. In their hearts they knew that they were simply strong enough to deal with even the pair of them as they saw fit; for certainly the man would not dare to draw a gun against them; but the perfect calm of Corcoran lay like a weight of dread upon their minds. They feared him, they knew not why. Something of his ominous reputation had already been buzzed at their ears, but, more than rumor, they were impressed by the dauntless indifference of the slender gambler. He walked on serenely, unhurried. The moment his back was turned they would have swarmed upon him and buried him under an avalanche of vigorous, fighting, squirming bodies; but behind him walked their arch-enemy — Willie. As well attempt to surprise a wild wolf as to take Willie off his guard. They had had one stroke of luck at his expense. They would never have another on that night!

So they allowed the two to get away down the alley. And Corcoran knew that the danger was over when the boy came up beside him.

"Jiminy, Mr. Corcoran," said Willie, "I thought we was done, for a minute."

"Frankly, so did I."

"I know," admitted the boy. "But you didn't know that you was scared and that was what beat 'em. Eh?"

"Perhaps."

"Mr. Corcoran, it was dog-gone fine of you to gimme a hand, like that. I ain't forgettin'. And — hey! Look out! Here she comes!"

"Who?" asked Corcoran.

Straight down the alley toward them hurried that same light, agile form of a girl which they had been following.

"It's her!" gasped out Willie, and turned to flee.

The slender hand of Corcoran darted out

and fixed upon the boy a grip as biting as iron.

"Who," he asked, "is her?"

"Miss Murran. You better not let her talk to you. She'll give you the dickens, Mr. Corcoran. And when she talks — it's a pile worse'n taking a beating!"

Miss Murran came swiftly up out of the gloom, but Corcoran held his wriggling prisoner safe. A meager shaft of light struck across her features as she approached and gave him a glimpse of a brown, pretty face. Certainly he had seen a hundred more beautiful girls, but there was something thrilling about her. The very way she carried her head with its cap and its curling fluff of bobbed hair and the round slender young throat made her more like a boy — and yet more sweetly feminine, too.

When she came close, she quickened her walk to a run. At the end of it she caught Willie away from Corcoran and into her arms. There was a startled gasp from the boy.

"Willie! Willie! Willie!" cried Miss Murran. "How dare you be so bad and terrible! I've told you *never* to follow me downtown! Have they hurt you, poor child? Have they beaten and bruised you terribly? Oh, the cowards! The little savages!"

She pushed Willie away to arm's length to examine him. It made Corcoran think of a gazelle solicitously caring for a fierce young wolf.

"Jiminy, Miss Murran," said the boy. "It wasn't nothin'. I ain't hurt. Nothin' happened. Mr. Corcoran came in and stopped them."

She kept one hand curled around the head of Willie, holding him close to her, while she went up to Corcoran and held out the other.

"I suppose we're introduced?" said she.

Corcoran bowed above that hand, taking it carefully in his own boney, sensitive fingers. Those finger tips of his could almost "read the mind of a pack of cards" as an envious rival had once said of him. Now they told him in the thick dark what the hand of the girl was — how slender it was, and how firmly and delicately made. What the hand is, the woman must be. It was an old maxim of Corcoran's. And holding her hand for the space of half a second, he saw her more clearly, perhaps, than if he met her a dozen times by daylight. Yet here all he could see was the faint outline of her face and the glimmering of her eyes. He was stabbed with a sharp regret — that she had not seen him for the first time with enough light to illustrate his elegance. Without his clothes he felt that he was only half himself. Such was the vanity of Corcoran!

"Willie," she was saying, "can you get home without running into any more trouble?"

"You ain't going to go to that Dorn place ag'in, are you?" asked Willie, who had managed to wriggle free at last.

"How do you know that I have ever been at the Dorn place before?" she asked.

"I dunno. I just —"

"Willie, you have followed me there before!"

"You see, Miss Murran!"

"Go home this instant, Willie! And if I hear that you've been fighting again —"

She broke off on a direful accent of threat.

"Might I say a word to Mr. Corcoran?" asked Willie meekly.

"Of course. Good night, Mr. Corcoran. Oh, Willie, please be a good boy!"

She was away down the alley again, and Willie clutched the arm of his companion. "Can you beat that?" he asked. "You never can figger what she'll do. I thought there'd be a terrible tongue lashin'. All she does is to gimme a hug. Jiminy!"

"She *is* odd," admitted Corcoran.

"She's got the world stopped," declared

Willie thoughtfully. "But she's so dog-gone busy tryin' to help folks that she'll get herself into a pile of trouble. These here Dorns — they ain't no good, Mr. Corcoran. Would you mind lookin' after her now? I don't dare to keep follering along after her now. She'd be so mad she'd plumb bust if she found out!"

"Will you do what she told you to do?"

"Well," said Willie, "it wouldn't do no harm if I was to cut off one or two of them while they was on their ways home. I mean, just to say a couple of words to 'em, Mr. Corcoran."

"Get along, you young viper," chuckled Corcoran. "But you'll have to move, Willie, for here they come sneaking up on you again!"

The band of Willie's enemies had by no means scattered after the failure of their first attempt against him on account of the interference of the gambler. But, hanging in the distance, ready to pursue the hostile force as soon as it should get under way, they now were stealing gradually near and nearer, taking post close to the fronts of the houses and keeping generally in the shadows everywhere.

As for Willie Kern, he turned his keen eye slowly here and there, regarding the forms of his enemies with a slight curling of his upper lip. Had he been a man, his bearing could have been called imperious; and in Willie it was at least a thing of pride. Corcoran watched him with a mingled concern and amusement.

"What if they catch you again?" he asked Willie.

In return, the boy reached into a capacious pocket and drew out a long, heavy knife. He pressed a spring and a four-inch blade snapped open. Standing dexterously poised upon one foot, still viewing his foemen as they crept nearer, he whetted the glistening blade upon the horny sole of his bare foot. Then he stowed the knife in his pocket again.

"If they was to mob me ag'in," said Willie, "I dunno but what I could give 'em something to think about, Mr. Corcoran."

A bit of advice came into the throat of the gambler, but he swallowed it again and shrugged his shoulders. He merely said: "There are a great many different ways of getting oneself hung, Willie. But are you sure that you don't need any help to get away? You can see that they've bottled you up by corking both ends of the alley."

"Say," said Willie, "I ain't a cripple!"

With that, he ran straight at the face of the

nearest house and, leaping high, planted his feet on the sill of the window, clutching the ledge above, and so in another moment had clambered like a monkey to the roof. There he paused and waved his hand mockingly toward the gang, which was closing after him with shouts of rage. Then he disappeared, running across the flat roof.

CHAPTER 11

Corcoran, hurrying on, came up with the girl in the street beyond. She made a pause just before he reached her, and then they went on side by side.

"I knew it was you," she said, "when I heard that light, quick step coming up behind me. Is it something about Willie?"

"He sent me to take care of you," said Corcoran. "One cannot disobey Willie, you know."

At this she laughed a little, and speaking or laughing, there was the same soft, rather husky quality in her voice, and it fascinated Corcoran like the taste of a strange fruit. They had come opposite the light from an open doorway in which squatted the Mexican man of the house with his good wife still drudging in the kitchen behind him. She used this opportunity to survey her companion, and Corcoran felt her eye run swiftly over him. He spun his cane and began to whistle a bar of music.

When he could take notice of her out of the corner of his eye, he saw that some of the bonhomie had gone out of her manner. She held herself a little more stiffly.

"She takes me," said Corcoran to his soul, "for a dandy."

At this, he began to chuckle soundlessly.

"You are very happy?" asked the girl.

"Very!"

"It *is* lovely," said she. "Sometimes the days are terribly brown and hot and sun-burned. But there are always the nights. If one could only sleep in the day and live at night — that would be a beautiful way, don't you think so Mr. Corcoran?"

"It's my usual practice," said he.

"Oh!" murmured she, and looked askance at him through the darkness.

He bit his lip. But there was nothing to be said in explanation. His wits were oddly be-numbed.

"Willie," he said, "is terribly worried about your interest in the Dorn family."

"I know," said the girl. "Mrs. Dorn is a forlorn old thing whose dead husband used to be rich. She is crumbling to pieces, now. Nerves and such things, you know. But she has a wonderful son."

"H-m-m!" said Corcoran without great enthusiasm.

"He really is a fine fellow," said the girl, throwing up her head after a way she had, and smiling at the stars. "All soul and fire; and so gentle and patient with his mother. He reads to her and nurses her. It is a beautiful thing to see him with her!"

"What does he do for a living?" asked Corcoran.

"A living? Well, he's an artist. He paints. And he writes, too. His work is just like Gabriel Dorn — beautiful, strange — like a dream, you know."

"Ah?" said Corcoran. "What does he paint?"

"Landscapes, mostly. He loves the desert and the mountains, you see. He's attuned to them."

Corcoran with a slash of his cane sabered a bunch of tall, dead grass which cropped up through a crack in the sidewalk.

"He makes enough to keep his mother, I suppose?" said he.

"Well, in a way," answered Kitty Murran. "That is to say — he makes as much as he can. A man can't do more than that, you know!"

"Perhaps he has friends who help him?"

"Well," said the girl, a little embarrassed, "I — I really don't know."

But Corcoran had heard enough. It would

be very odd indeed if she were not helping the artist out of her own small salary.

"Here's the house," she said, as they came on the outskirts of San Pablo to a miserable dobe hut.

"May I come in with you?" asked Corcoran.

She hesitated a little. "I don't think you'd better. They — they're not equipped to meet many people at once, and poor Mrs. Dorn —"

"I understand," said Corcoran.

"Are you to be in San Pablo long?"

"I don't know. I rather think so."

"Oh," she said. "I'm might glad of that! For the sake of Willie, you know. He feels that you're the greatest man he's ever met, Mr. Corcoran. And I hope I'll see you again. Good night!"

She turned in through the front gate, and there she paused, working to replace the pivot which had fallen out of its socket. Corcoran, walking around the corner, found himself shut at once from her view, and at this, he leaped lightly over the fence and ran to the side of the house.

There was only a single room, so that his glance through the window revealed the whole interior. It was like a scene from a junk shop. In one corner was the stove, with the pots and pans hanging on the wall and something stewing at that moment over the fire. In another corner stood a large easel with a half finished picture display — something done in the large manner of the ultra modern school, with thick, broad sweeps of the brush, and representing a desert scene, a flush of sunset, and against it a coyote howling at the moon which hung in mid-heaven like a wisp of silver cloud. The idea was old enough; but the execution was wholly new and wholly bad. So much the gambler could tell at a glance.

Two cots in opposite corners supplied sleeping quarters, and at a rickety table in the center of the apartment sat mother and son indulging in a game of cribbage, supporting their spirits in fortune and misfortune by generous swigs from a tall black jug which stood at the flank of the cribbage board. They were opposites in physical feature. She was a dowdy blonde of vast proportions, with a pasty pale face and flabby jowls, her loose body now wrapped in a Mother Hubbard, and her hair pasted in streaks against her perspiring face. The artist was a thin-faced fellow with big black eyes and a sallow skin, and the fingers of his hands were like long, thin talons of a bird of prey.

Here they heard the tap of the front door and the voice of the teacher calling out to them. They exchanged broad grins. Then each fell to work with the greatest agility. Mrs. Dorn heaved herself out of her chair and waddled to her bed on which she disposed herself hastily, drawing the spread over her ample body and fluffing up her hair, while she hastily caught up a book and lighted a lamp with a smoked chimney which stood on the bedside table.

Her son was even more active. With lightning gestures he made the whiskey jug and the cribbage board disappear. Next he cast a paint-smudged apron around his skinny body, rumpled his stiff black hair until it was standing half on end and in the wildest disarray, and scooped up a paint brush.

In this guise he appeared as he opened the door for Kitty Murran and bowed her into the room. She gave him a smile which made the heart of Corcoran leap. Then she went straight to Mrs. Dorn. That good woman greeted her with a sad, patient smile, as of one who has endured much from life and must still endure more. With a gesture of resignation, as who should say that her own state was too bad to be helped she pointed across the room to where her son stood before the picture with his legs spread wide, busily brushing in a cloud in mid-heaven, its under side flushed with gold.

So Kitty Murran went to the painter. Corcoran saw her hands clasped, and heard the note of her cry of admiration. The artist received her adulation with the impatient gesture of one who cannot be disturbed in the midst of inspiration. But he stood back, presently, and clasping one hand against his brow began to point out his effect with his brush.

Corcoran could wait to see no more. It was all so tawdry, so ridiculous, that he gritted his teeth and went away. He leaped the fence and went down the sidewalk with a halting step, pausing frequently with a groan of shame and anger at what he had seen. The slender cane was no longer dapperly poised, but he gripped it in one hard hand and went on with his jaw set.

He went back to the main street and inquired for the sheriff. He was directed to that worthy at once. It was plain that San Pablo kept an eye on honest Mike Nolan as much as Nolan kept an eye on San Pablo.

"Back again?" said the sheriff. "And lookin' dog-gone thoughtful."

"I have been thinking over what you had to say, sheriff. And I've decided to stay quite a time in San Pablo."

"You're a bold man, Corcoran," said the sheriff. "I'll hope that you don't come to no harm by stayin'. You nor me!"

"In fact," said Corcoran. "I've decided to stay with safety for both of us."

"I'm a tolerable old man," said the sheriff, "but dog-gone me if you don't make me feel kind of young and foolish. How'd you aim to manage that, Corcoran?"

"I'll tell you, sheriff. It can be done by leaving my revolver behind me. Will that meet your idea of safety?"

The sheriff merely blinked. "Partner," he said, "it sure looks to me as if you're talkin' for the sake of hearin' yourself talk."

Corcoran drew out his revolver. How easily, how smoothly it glided forth in his hand.

"Take it," he said to the sheriff.

The sheriff extended a brown paw for it, gingerly, as though he were accepting as a present a can of cold nitroglycerine. He held it before him almost at arm's length.

"There ain't nothin' to bar you from havin' two guns," he said at length.

"You can search me if you wish."

"I'll take your word, son. Corcoran, what's got into you? What sort of joke is this?"

"It's straight talk, sheriff."

"They's forty men in town that ain't got no love for you, Corcoran."

"I'll have to learn how to smile," was the answer of the gambler.

"Very well. Corcoran, what's happened to you?"

"I've reformed," said Corcoran. "Because I can't live in the same town with you unless I change my pace. So long, sheriff."

"He's deep and smooth," said the sheriff to himself as he watched the slender form of the gambler disappear through the night. "But this time he's talkin' the truth. They's only two things could of happened to him. Is it religion, or is it a woman? Poor devil!"

The grief of the sheriff and his sympathy was expressed in a sight which came from his heart.

CHAPTER 12

He who fears to be burned should avoid fire, of course, and the firm resolution of Thomas Naseby Corcoran was to shun gaming houses while he stayed in San Pablo. He had gone to the root of danger by giving up his gun. He who is conscious that his strength is with him is apt to use it, as Corcoran was well aware. And now, as he strolled down the street, he told himself that he had turned a new page in his career. But just as that resolve crystallized in his thoughts, he came opposite the blaze of two powerful gasoline lamps and saw enshrined in the illumination the following sign:

Ted Rankin's Place
THE SKY IS THE LIMIT

He brooded over it with a gleaming eye. With his nervous finger tips he pressed the breast of his coat and took the comfortable feeling of the thick wad of bank notes which filled the wallet that was concealed there.

Ted Rankin's place might have been compared to a domed Roman temple fronted by a Doric portico. That is to say, the original building was a low-faced Spanish structure of dobe in which the Goddess of Chance had presided during several generations before it fell into the ambitious hands of Theodore Rankin. He had hardly taken possession when the gold strike of Comanche Mountain multiplied the prosperity of San Pablo by ten. Mr. Rankin was not of a nature to allow such an opportunity to slip through his grasping, fat fingers. He promptly knocked out the rear wall of his building and annexed to it a huge circus tent which swelled in a vast white dome behind the dobe structure and above it. Under this tent he housed various amusement devices. As, for instance, he installed a dance-hall section with an orchestra which was chiefly distinguished for its brass instruments; he established a restaurant which was quite the best in town and in which the prices were doubled. But what miner with gold in his pocket cares for prices? If one did not dine in Rankin's, at San Pablo, it could not be said that one had lived out the day properly. And your true Westerner is a stickler for form.

113

This is a truth which is not often appreciated. But cowboy fashions are as fixed and as rigid as steel, whether dress, manners, or speech are considered. West of the Rockies a man would rather chop off a hand than appear in an unexpected article of clothing or be caught using precise English. To be manly, one must be ungrammatical, say the canons of good behavior as they are accepted in the mountain desert. The rare force of Corcoran was simply that he broke the rule. So it was that Ted Rankin's, having become the fashion, was "made." There were other gambling institutions in the town, but Rankin's was the flower among them all. For a dollar lost in the others, four were lost under the roof of this dobe or his tent. And the noise of his orchestra passed humming through the town. When all the winds were still, one could hear it even on the farthest verge of San Pablo.

Some of these things were unknown to Corcoran, but he guessed them all before he had been standing half a minute in front of the entrance to the gambling place. He could tell the habitués of the place by the reckless confidence of the winners and the grim determination of the losers who knew that to-night the luck must turn. He could tell the newcomers by the half nervous, half gay expectation with which they passed through the doors, their eyes glittering suspiciously to the right and to the left. Corcoran observed these things and the numbers who flowed in and the few who came out. There was money in that place. There was much money. It was richer than the mines of Comanche Mountain; and very, very little of the precious stuff was allowed to escape!

Then, taking himself firmly in hand, he spun his cane and sauntered on. A jeering, laughing, half drunken cow-puncher, pointing out the dude to his companions, shouldered the gambler before he had taken half a dozen steps, and Corcoran slashed him across the face with the slender ebony stick. The fellow leaped away, half blinded, and reached for his gun, but a dozen hands of his friends mastered him at once.

"You fool! That's Corcoran!"

How sweet, how sweet to the spirit of Corcoran were those words!

He went on half a hundred paces with music in his soul. Then something stopped him. He fought against it. But, after all, there was no harm in looking at the place again, or in watching the people drift in through the doors. He returned and stood to gaze. It was cowardice to be so unsure of himself as to shun the very face of temptation. So he passed on through the entrance.

Music blared at him from the dance hall. A swirl of hurrying cow-punchers caught him up and wafted him like a dead leaf into a big chamber roofed with canvas and walled with rough, unpainted pine. Even that timber had cost a small fortune! All was very primitive. Stout tree trunks, blazed with white where the branches had been lopped off, were sunk in the ground and their heads bore up the canvas, and from their sides hung literally scores of clean lanterns. One could see well enough to read a newspaper in every corner of the place except where certain thick shadows streaked to the side. The floor needed no deadening to cover the sound of footfalls; it consisted merely of the hard-packed earth, moistened thrice a day to keep it from working into dust. In the central space were the roulette wheels and other devices where crowds could play. But Corcoran paid no attention to these places. They are for those who wished to blindly sue cruel Fortune; for his own part, he had no such ambition. He knew that lady far too well for any such frivolous viewpoint. His interest centered in the little tables which were scattered around the edges of the room.

The steady drone of music died away at the end of a dance and from the dance hall he heard the sharp laughter of girls, the booming notes of men's voices. But in the gaming hall there was never more than a subdued murmuring. Men said nothing as they laid their wagers, or asked for their cards in muffled tones as though they feared that a loud voice would guide bad luck to them.

"Corcoran, by heaven!" said a nasal voice beside him.

He looked down into the meager face of "Skinny" Montague, that Bedouin of the gaming tables.

"Somebody passed me the tip that you were in town, Corcoran," said the little man, his rat eyes gleaming up to his companion. "I knew with all this honey floating around loose that the queen bee would blow in after a while. Where are you going to sit, Corcoran? Are you fixed up for a partner? If you ain't —"

He made a slight gesture. Plainly he was willing to play crooked cards with such a master for a partner.

"What sort of a place?" asked Corcoran.

"Pretty straight, except where they pull the big stuff. Darned straight, except where they take the limit off."

"Where's that?"

He was shown to a round table in a corner at which two men sat idling.

"That fat beef with the red face — that's Rankin. I'll introduce you."

He kept on chattering softly from the crooked corner of his mouth as they advanced.

"That big fellow is one of Rankin's best men. A darned hard one, too. I warn you, Corcoran. Anything goes at that table. Every trick in the game is on deck and O.K. Only a question of who can pull the deepest stuff, and get away with it. And there ain't anybody yet who's been able to put it ever on Joe Cracken."

"Is that Joe Cracken?" asked Corcoran, fixing his glance on the solemn, sad face of the famous gambler. "Skinny, I'll try to make a game of it over there. But I'll play by myself, if you don't mind."

"Sure," said Skinny with a sigh.

Half a minute later: "Mr. Rankin, Mr. Cracken — I want you to meet Tom Corcoran, my friend. I guess you've heard of him."

The eyes of Rankin rolled in his fat face, as he rose to shake hands, and there his heart failed him, for he saw a sudden grayness pass over his professional gambler's face. Cracken was afraid, and very much afraid. And if Cracken began to lose — then heaven help Rankin, for at this table, the sky was the limit, and the fact that such a table existed in his house was his chief advertisement. In the hands of Cracken, it had also been his chiefest source of income. "I'm not playing," said Corcoran, "I just looked in."

The heart of Rankin beat again.

"What?" cried Montague. He added in a sharp, savage whisper: "They're comin' over to watch you work. They'll say that you're yaller if you don't play. They'll say that you're scared to match Cracken —"

Corcoran had taken into his mind the picture of Kitty Murran and held the thought of her like a fragrance charming his heart to good — like another Odysseus holding a magic flower to preserve him from enchantment. But this speech of Montague struck the fresh, happy face out of his brain. He glanced hastily behind him. There they came, to be sure, eager, forgetful of their own games, ready to watch a master at work. A score of men were drifting toward the table at which "the sky is the limit." Conscience pulled strongly on Corcoran and all of his new resolves; but pride drew him fully as strongly in the opposite direction. He had lived his life as though on a stage. Here he was in the center behind the footlights. The curtain had risen upon him. The audience was hushed in expectation. Could he walk off the boards like a dolt, without having uttered so much as a single line spoken?

"Suppose I take a hand or two?" he muttered. "I can only stay a minute. I have another engagement —"

And he slipped into a chair!

At that moment it seemed to him that the ghost of the girl stood up before him on the farther side of the table and faded away into the distance looking at him with reproachful eyes.

CHAPTER 13

Theodore Rankin saw before him a grave crisis in his financial life. He saw, indeed, the possibility of ruin. It was not that he particularly feared Corcoran. So far as he knew, there was no one in the world who was really superior to Joe Cracken in the manipulation of the cards. Perhaps Joe Cracken had hardly less faith in himself as a cheat. But there was another point of importance. Dexterous as Cracken was with cards, he was hardly less so with his gun. He was almost equally famous for both qualities. When he sat at a table, he was not taking chances; he was simply putting in his time digging gold. Yet skillful as he was with weapons, there now sat before him one who, according to the swift tongue of rumor, was a matchless warrior. He had sat before other famous gunmen; but as a rule he who is clever with a heavy Colt revolver has calloused fingers, and as all followers of crooked cards know, a pack cannot be manipulated with stiff fingers. All must be suppleness, liquid ease. And there were the hands of Corcoran resting on the edge of the table — slender, delicately made hands, almost trembling with the possibilities of nervous speed.

Joe Cracken had faced many a great fighter across the card table. He had faced many an expert gambler. But he had never before encountered such a consummate admixture of both as was represented by Corcoran, and his nerve was shaken. He tried to mask his lack of ease behind a smile. He tried to rest and to steady his nerve by forcing his glance slowly across the semicircle of watching faces. But no matter how steady a face he kept, he was hollow with weakness within. And poor Ted Rankin saw and understood. No matter how skillful his hired gambler might be, the skill of Cracken would be turned to nothing by his dread lest Corcoran should detect him, and lest such detection should lead to a gun play.

Already, perhaps, the uneasy glance of Cracken was probing the slender figure of Corcoran, wondering where the gun was concealed, within the belt of the trousers or under the armpit, perhaps?

Rankin was seized with a sudden coughing fit which swayed him to the side and made him cover his face with his hand.

In a brief interval between the coughing spasms, he whispered swiftly to his man: "Let Corcoran win a couple of hands. Then maybe he'll pull out. For Heaven's sake, get yourself together!"

He wished, instantly, that he had not spoken. The pallor of Cracken had increased. The knowledge that his fear was visible to any eye had filled him with panic. If Rankin saw, would Corcoran fail to see?

No, the steady, gray eye of Corcoran never left his face. It was not a confident and insolent stare. It was merely a bloodless glance of inquiry. It was a knifelike probing which never ceased, and poor Cracken set his teeth to endure it.

The game was lost before it began. Rankin saw Corcoran push five hundred dollars onto the table to bet on the first hand. And in his soul of souls he groaned. It made no difference that Corcoran won. He put fifteen hundred dollars in cold cash on the very next wager, while the crowd grew hushed, witnessing such play as this. Rankin rose from the table with a sick face, and went away with feeble and fumbling steps. He felt old and very ill. He wanted to ask for sympathy like a child. But the face of every man who watched the game was the face of a fox. They wanted blood, Rankin's blood. They wanted the house to lose.

So Rankin went back to his private room and sat down with everything whirling around him, like a landscape before the eyes of a drunkard. Stevens was in his room, as usual — Stevens, his confidential man, his spy, the rat that had gnawed into many an important secret, the yellow-skinned, sneering devil. Stevens, who lived like a parasite on Rankin because he had lost his own gaming nerve.

"Go watch Cracken," breathed the master of the house.

"What's happened?"

"Corcoran!"

"And Cracken's showed yellow?"

"Get out, darn you! Go watch the game!"

Stevens disappeared. He came back in five minutes.

"Well?" gasped out Rankin.

"It's all up."

Great beads of perspiration oozed out on the forehead of Rankin. He drank from a silver flask and put it down again on the table against which it clattered in his shaking hand.

"What d'you mean?" he managed to gasp out.

"It's only five thousand," said Stevens, looking tactfully at the floor so as to keep his eye from the collapse of his master. "But Cracken is done for. He's white as a piece of paper. He has nothing on the cards to-night. And Corcoran is making them talk for him. He's a devil!"

Theodore Rankin collapsed in his chair with a moan. There he lay, the outlines of his body dissolved and turned into a quivering mass of fat, his wide, loose mouth sagging open.

"Five thousand — already!" he exclaimed, and the thought jerked him upright again.

"Get Joe Cracken in here with me!" he snarled out.

The other blinked. "Quit the game? It'll queer your house, chief!"

"Don't yap at me, you fool. Go get Cracken. Get Cracken. Quick. It — it may be ten thousand by now! He can excuse himself for five minutes, can't he? That's allowed, ain't it? Run, you coyote, and tip him the wink!"

Stevens disappeared from the office. He was gone for only a few minutes, but that was time enough for Ted Rankin to seize a cigar, in front of which, lost in thought, he allowed a match to burn to the quick of his finger tips. He dropped it, hurled the cigar upon the earthen floor, and stamped it into a black, oily, shapeless mass. He caught up another, lighted it, and had chewed the mouthpiece to rage before the quick step of Stevens and the long stride of Cracken approached.

The gambler came in, haggard and worn, with the look of an athlete at the end of a Marathon race. Rankin stood before him, shuddering with rage.

"You've quit on me, Cracken!" he snarled. "You've quit on me, you — you —"

"Easy!" said the big man, reaching a significant hand toward his hip. But there was no conviction in his tone. He turned to the flask which stood on the table, partly for the drink, partly to get from the accusing eyes of his boss. He tipped up the flask in an uncertain hand and drained half the contents. Then he was able to face Rankin again.

"I ain't quitting," he said, muttering. "But this Corcoran has something new on the cards. He's reading their minds. I don't savvy it. That's all."

"You don't? You don't savvy it? The devil, Cracken, everybody in the house knows that you've opened up a yellow streak a mile wide!"

Even a beaten horse must not be lashed too freely, particularly if there is a dash of wild mustang blood in it. The long, heavy hand of Cracken fastened in the pudgy throat of Rankin and crushed him into a chair.

"You fat pup — I'll step on you — I'll squash you!" said Cracken through his teeth. "Keep away from me, Stevens. Or I'll finish you next!"

Stevens had reached for a coward's weapon — his knife. Here was his opportunity to deliver a signal service to his master. But though the spirit was willing, the flesh was weak. He could not draw the knife forth. And against the door he cowered weakly, cursing himself and his own cowardice in an hysterical whisper, but unable to nerve himself to action.

Rankin saw and snarled with disgust. There was no physical fear in his fat body. It was only the thought of losing money which had crushed him and then maddened him. Now he writhed against the choking hand and spat forth his insults, undaunted.

Finally Cracken stood back, lowering, red faced. He was breathing hard, and it was apparent that this exercise of his own strength had reassured him of his own prowess, so to speak. He had been blooded, and now was ready to kill. His black eyes glittered at the owner of the place.

"You fat bum," he said unpoetically,

"I've dealt my last game for you!"

But though the throat of Rankin ached
and was bruised to a dark purple by the gripping fingers of the other, and though his
shirt was torn and his necktie pulled far to
one side, he felt for the moment no raging
personal resentment. After all, the insults he
had used had been only intended as a stimulus. Now that the stimulus was so mani-
festly working, he wanted only to take
advantage of it before it wore out. His establishment was on the verge of ruin. At the
table where "the sky was the limit," a hole
was being bored which might let in the sea.
And, when that happened, there was an end
to the fortune of Ted Rankin. He was desperate. He must use some tool to beat off
Corcoran, and the only available man was
his gambler. That game must be ended.
And that was his goal from the first.

"Partner," he said, gripping the arm of
the big man, an arm stiff and quivering with
the taut, angry muscles, "I was just working
you up, Joe. I knew you had the stuff in you.
But I wanted to wake you up!"

"You did? You darn near got yourself put
to sleep at the same time," answered
Cracken, still fierce.

"Maybe — maybe — now listen,
Cracken, we're done if that game goes on.

I'm done. He'll clean me out. He'll push the stakes up. Money's nothing to a devil like Corcoran. He'll bet a million if he gets a chance. I can't stand the gaff the way he'll work it. There's only one chance. You got to stop that game!"

"Me?" muttered Cracken, his eyes wild as he began to guess at what was coming.

"If it ruins me, it'll ruin you, too, Joe. They're all watching you, ain't they?"

"There ain't nothing stirring in the whole house," answered Cracken. "They've cut out the dancing. The orchestra has laid up. Darned if they ain't all swarming around my table — watching! The devil and damnation, that's what bothers me. They're smashing my game to bits!"

"Maybe — maybe — but if you lose this here game, if Corcoran goes on and cleans you and me out, d'you know that you'll never get a chance to work in another house? D'you know why? D'you know why you won't?"

"Don't say it, Rankin!" snapped out the big fellow, groaning.

Rankin retreated, but he muttered through his teeth: "They're saying that you're yellow, Joe. Yellow. You hear me? *Yellow!*"

Cracken folded his arms. "I've used up all

my patience," he said. "Don't say that again, old-timer. They's a red mist all hangin' in front of me!"

"Look, Joe, for Heaven's sake! You got only one chance. They's only one way of stopping that game."

"I guess I know — but — say it!"

"You got to stop Corcoran."

"You want him killed?" asked Cracken huskily.

"The devil, man, do I want to be a beggar? D'you want to get yourself queered?"

Cracken was silent, staring at the floor.

"Go back and do it now. On his deal — call the first card he plays. Don't give him no chance to get to workin' on you with those funny eyes of his. Just call his turn and pull a gat and start in shootin'. You understand, old-timer? When you're still hot. Before you get all froze up again."

"I kill Corcoran — or I get killed. Either way stops that game. You win both ways, Rankin. What do *I* win?"

"You get your reputation back. You stop the dirty mouths that are beginning to yap about you."

"That'll do! Reputation is all right to talk about. I'll take a chance on that. What I want to know is — what am I workin' for? What am I playin' for?"

Rankin caught his arm again and hurried him toward the door. "Don't talk foolish. You know me, Cracken."

"Sure. I ain't drunk."

"You know that I'll take care of you, then."

"I tell you, I ain't drunk, Rankin. I want to hear some talk. I'm wide awake."

"Well — turn the trick and you're in a thousand, old son!"

"I said I wasn't drunk. Don't you believe me, Rankin? Think I'm drunk and a fool, too?"

"Look here, Joe. A cool thousand ain't enough? You know me. My purse is always open. I don't strike no easy bargains. Make it two thousand. Do the work and you collect two thousand."

"Listen, Rankin. This is Corcoran that you're talkin' about shuttin' off."

"I know it. What's Corcoran? What's he? He ain't the devil, is he?"

"He's a first cousin to him, though. I'd rather pat a rattlesnake than play tag with guns with that gent. He ain't nice, Rankin. He's bad as the devil — that's all!"

"Three thousand, Joe. Three thousand cold simoleons!"

Cracken shrugged his shoulders. Then he sat down and shook his head.

"Good heavens!" cried Rankin. "You want me to pay you as much as I'd lose to Corcoran if the game went on?"

"Don't talk foolish, man, because this here Corcoran ain't warmed up yet. He's won about seven thousand. But he plays like money was just dirt to him. I mean that! He throws it around. You can't bust the heart of a gent like that. You can't stir him up. He's ice. That's all. Ice!" added the gambler savagely to his own bitterly envious heart. "What'll you lose to Corcoran? He'll keep on till he's got every penny you have. You were a fool to ever start that 'sky-limit' stuff. I told you so. It made you money. Now it'll cook your hash."

All the enthusiasm was leaving Rankin as he saw that he could not rush the big fellow into that fight. He began to puff at his cigar until the fire, which had died down to a spark in one corner of the tobacco, spread suddenly across the whole face of the butt and began to burn in a slanted line, eating fast into the heart of the cigar. The room was filled with jagged wreaths of smoke.

"Well," he snapped out over his shoulder, as he paced back and forth, "what do you want?"

"Ten thousand berries. That'll about do me."

Rankin halted sharply, still with his back to the other. "You ain't crazy, Joe?"

"Ten thousand, old son. I got one chance in five, about."

"You're lightning with a gun."

"Corcoran is lightninger."

That thought decided the proprietor. He sat down to the table and drew out a gold fountain pen.

"Write her this way," said Cracken. "If Cracken stops the game between him and Corcoran, I promise to pay eight thousand dollars —"

The cigar tilted sharply upward in the corner of Rankin's mouth as he set his teeth. Then the pen scratched hastily across the sheet.

CHAPTER 14

In that long pause which had occupied the crowd in the gaming house during the interval after Cracken had momentarily excused himself from the game, Corcoran was perfectly at home. Nearly every person in the entire establishment had gathered as near as possible to watch. Here and there a small group of men sat at a side table entranced in poker, oblivious of the rest of the world. But the others had forgotten that which had interested them before; a great raid was being made on Ted Rankin's bank. Within the hour, the whole place might be lost.

Crises gather an electric atmosphere. Men feel them almost before they knew them. And the news had been wirelessed without a word to the front door of Rankin's, and to the passing crowd on the street. Dozens of passers-by were sucked into the entrance, hardly knowing why they came. Mexicans, Indians, half-breeds, Negroes, sun-blackened miners, and white-faced gamesters came flocking in, gathering slowly and steadily on the outskirts of the crowd. And the focus of all attention was the slender form of Corcoran.

He enjoyed it with all his heart. The stage was set, and he occupied the center of it. Now and then a small shadow darted across his mind. To-morrow Kitty Murran would know that he was a gambler. But, for that matter, he was notorious and must become known to her in spite of this evening's work. So he put those shadows away.

In the meantime, he sat a little sidewise at the table, smoking, and making himself sublimely unconscious of those who stood around him, but drinking in admiration and catching a few of their loudest whispers. He finished his cigarette and dandled his cane between his fingers.

"Roland is back!" said a sudden voice behind him.

"Not Henry Roland!"

"It's him. I see him over the heads of the crowd. He's big enough to be seen."

There was a stir, a general giving back by mutual assent, and the stranger came close to the table. He had not spoken a word, and yet of itself the crowd had made place for him. From the corner of his eye, with furtive, careless glances, Corcoran studied a tall fellow, young, very handsome, with a fine, square jaw and a smile that brought deep dimples into his cheeks. Not that there was anything effeminate about that smile; rather, it accentuated his essential manliness. One noted it in contrast with the bold black-eyes which had a trick of dwelling a little too long and fixedly on whatever face they touched. He was dressed like a man of property accoutered for roughing it, with high pigskin boots which laced more than halfway up the calves of his legs, a broad sombrero, and a plain flannel shirt. Every one else in the room, well nigh, had togged himself forth in his best. But Henry Roland was too sure of himself. He could afford to dress down to the occasion rather than up to it. He had done Rankin's grace by putting on smart bow tie. That was all.

He surveyed the natty garb of Corcoran with a quiet smile of amusement. "Some one introduce me," he said to the people around him. "I want to meet Corcoran."

A gliding, stealthy form had made its way through the thick of the crowd. It was Stevens, returning, and he heard the request. He was always glad to take any small office upon himself.

"Corcoran," he said, "stand up and meet Mr. Henry Roland."

Corcoran turned slowly in his chair and surveyed the stranger frankly. Roland had politely sobered his expression. Now Corcoran rose without haste and extended his slender hand. The big, vigorous fist of the other closed over it. Their eyes met firmly, searchingly, and each knew the other — one a gentleman who had fallen from his right estate, one a man whose honor was still bright and clean. Some of the color left the face of Corcoran, and though he managed a smile as he sat down again, half of his assurance was gone. His foppish dress suddenly seemed both theatrical and foolish. It was cheap; it cheapened the very soul of Corcoran.

"We've met before," big Roland was saying.

Corcoran started a little and stared fixedly at the other. "I never forget faces," he said coldly and pointedly.

It seemed that Roland was too important to take offense easily. He merely shrugged the implication from his broad shoulders. "I was wearing a head guard and a crimson jersey," said he in answer.

The whole body of Corcoran quivered. Twice before he had encountered men who were familiar with his college career, but in each instance his changed name, and his occupation had been enough to shelter him from observance. But now he merely murmured: "Ah?" and produced his cigarette case, which he held out.

Roland took one, fumbling for it, never taking his eyes from the face of Corcoran, as though he could not leave off the story which he was reading there.

When they spoke again, it was through a mist of smoke, which Roland was constantly brushing away.

"I went in at right half back in the last five minutes of the game. It was my sophomore year. It was your senior year — in the Blue."

The eyes of Corcoran flashed up in silent gratitude because the name of the college had been omitted. Roland, suddenly, had become almost boyish, eager. What a gap of years was bridged! And how long had it been since he talked with such a man — there was hardly need of words between them. They knew one another. They were the same breed and bone and blood of men; except that the years had stained Corcoran, while the other had remained clean.

He stared at Roland, trying to remember.

"The quarterback plugged me through the line a couple of times. It was a new trick to you fellows in blue. The second crack was a first down," said Roland.

How it all swept back on the mind of Corcoran, now! The last game of his last year, his own body battered and broken by three seasons of football, only a shattered wreck of a once great team to rally behind him as their captain in this most important game of all, and how the great Crimson machine had rolled relentlessly down the field time after time, only to be checked by a miracle in the shadow of the goal posts — raving Crimson bleachers yelling for a touchdown, for blood — screaming Blue rooters, begging their team to hold off a score — and then in the last few minutes a new man in the Crimson backfield, an unknown, a plunging, tearing, devastating projectile of a man who crushed the Blue line to bits and drove on toward the goal. How his knees had sagged with weariness! How he had yelled at his reeling guards and tackles to fight destruction back! All in vain, until at the end of a scrimmage, he had said tauntingly to the youth in crimson: "Try my end, youngster!"

Ah, he remembered it well enough now!

"After that," Roland was saying, "I begged the quarter to send me around your end. It hadn't been passed for two whole seasons; he said I was crazy, but I was full of confidence, and at last he gave me a chance.

Do you remember?"

The heart of Corcoran was thundering; but he shook his head.

"It started perfectly," said Roland. "There were three husky fellows driving ahead of me as interference. I thought nothing could stop that landslide. Then a little streak in blue ducked between their legs, slid along the ground, and dropped me with a crash. That was you, Corcoran. Then I came to, and sat up. I saw the boys tearing down the field, chasing a chap in a Blue jersey — I'd dropped the ball! Do you remember now? You were lying under me — broken to bits. I picked you up. I remember you were groaning: 'I've missed! I've missed at last!' But you hadn't missed. You'd won the game for those lucky Blue devils!"

Yes, yes — Corcoran remembered. But it was sweet to have it told again. He remembered more. He recalled his bed in the hospital, and the newspapers, and his picture in them, and how the college president had sat at his side and said great things of what a heart of courage meant to the world and of the career which lay before him as a worthy son of the Blue.

Alas, the name which had been his was gone. Better, far better that he himself should be forgotten. He steeled himself and looked up to big Henry Roland.

"A very stirring story," he said. "But I'm sorry I can't lay claim to the hero's part. Must have been another man, Mr. Roland. There are these strange resemblances, you know."

He saw Roland staring at him. Was it all scorn, or was there some pity in his black eyes also?

"Quite so," said Roland stiffly. "Now that I look more closely, I see that I have been mistaken in you — Corcoran!"

There was a little murmur of regret about the circle of the listening crowd. Here was a touch of romance rubbed away — a pleasant story ruined. Then all of this was forgotten.

"Cracken!" said some one. And the gambler, striding to the table, dropped into his chair once more.

Plainly he was a changed man. He had been on the verge of nervous collapse, Corcoran knew, when the game was interrupted. But now Cracken was quite changed. His face was flushed, his eyes were bold, his manner savagely confident. His pungent breath afforded one explanation; he had reënforced himself with alcohol.

What fools men were to drink before they went hunting trouble, thought Corcoran. And then he remembered that he had given up his gun to the sheriff! The lack of it struck him weak with dismay. He looked again at the other. There could be no doubt of it. Cracken meant ugly work. Devilishness was printed black on his face.

It was Corcoran's deal. The game was blackjack. He flicked the cards out with a supple wrist, with fingers working so lightning fast that no eye could follow them.

If only the cold eye of Big Roland could be removed from the background! But in spite of that he must do his work.

A thousand hours of practice stood him in stead now. He was reading the cards three deep as he dealt; and he was burying the ones he did not wish to deal under the bottom card, which flashed face up with every card he let fall — a false assurance that all was well. Other men would not have been able to believe it; to cheat under those circumstances — to manipulate a pack with only one hand — that was black magic. Nevertheless, it was the stock in trade of Corcoran.

The last card fell. Then he was aware of Cracken rising slowly from the table, quivering like an angry, desperate beast, crouching a little, his right hand hidden behind him. Corcoran, rising in turn, did not need to be told that the fingers of his opponent were clutched about the butt of a revolver. Neither did the others in the room require to be told.

"Here it comes!" gasped out some one.

And the whole circle shrank back. Those in line with the foemen scrambled wildly to get out of the possible path of bullets. But it was only the disturbance of a moment. Here was a scene which they were willing to risk death to watch. Not a syllable that was spoken must escape them.

This was what happened in the first second as Corcoran rose, knowing that his hands were empty and that death was three feet away from him!

"Corcoran!" breathed Joe Cracken with a strange little whine in his voice.

Corcoran, slowly, deliberately — for a hasty move meant instant destruction — raised his ebony stick and rested its tips against the palms of his two hands. Both those hands were now in view, obviously unemployed with any weapon.

"Well?" said Corcoran.

"That last card — it looked to me — like — it was a queer deal, Corcoran!"

Corcoran strove in vain to catch his eye. For the glance of big Joe was like the look of a hungry brute, shifting constantly, intent on the body of his enemy into which he intended to drive his bullet, flicking across the face of the dapper gambler, but never daring for an instant to encounter the quiet magic of his eyes.

If he had his gun now — how simple it would be! The life of Cracken would be in the palm of his hand. He would not even have to kill. A bullet through the right shoulder. That would be enough!

"Well, Cracken," said he, "I don't pretend to understand you."

The fighting fury took Cracken by the throat and made his voice wild. "I say you're crooked as the devil! I saw you crook that last card, you —" His body tipped a little to one side. His teeth glinted between his stretched lips, and half of the ready Colt came into view. Then Corcoran found a thing to do.

He turned his back deliberately upon Joe Cracken, still with his ebony stick between his hands.

"It seems," said he, "that Ted Rankin doesn't like to lose. I'll call later for what I have won."

He spun the cane in his graceful right hand and forced his glance slowly across the faces of those who stood in front of him. Then he spoke, coolly, and in a way that commanded attention.

"Gentlemen," he said, "some of you will see that the money on the table is put in a bag and kept until tomorrow at noon. By that time I shall expect to meet Cracken, or Ted Rankin — or both — in the main street of the town. The hotel veranda would be an excellent place, I think. We can settle our little argument then. In the meantime — I make it a rule never to draw a gun on a drunkard."

They drew back and made a path before him — a clear way through the solidly packed mass of humanity. He felt their eyes plucking at his face. He felt their eyes before him and behind. He felt the wonder and the fear. Even the painted girls had forgotten how to smile and stared stupidly out of their old-young eyes.

Then he stood in the open. The street seemed empty. The wind was wonderfully cool on his face; its whisper was like a human voice; and above him the long white rays of the stars sliding through the infinite black heaven. He was alive, and it seemed the veriest miracle.

A big form hurried up behind him: a great hand fell upon his shoulder; he looked into the radiant face of Henry Roland.

"By the heavens, old fellow, that was magnificent."

"You do me too much credit," answered Corcoran. "I didn't have a gun with me, you see."

"Do you mean that? By the heavens, that's more wonderful still. I tell you Burling—"

"You continue to make an odd mistake," said Corcoran.

Roland drew himself suddenly to his height. "I beg your pardon, Mr. Corcoran," said he.

"Certainly," said Corcoran, and went on down the street slowly, touching the sidewalk delicately with the tip of the ebony cane.

CHAPTER 15

*٠٭٭٠٭

He was in no hurry to go into the hotel. The open night was like a beautiful face above him. Now the moon was there and the stars dared come no nearer to her than the edges of the horizon, where they shone faint and small; now the moon drove through the silver, ghostly seas of a rack of clouds, and as she grew dim the stars stole out again, higher and higher, until they were clustering at the very side of the queen of the heavens.

On the whole, he was very well pleased with himself. Take it all in all, the peril in which he had stood had been more extreme than any other in his life, for he had never before been actually helpless in the face of danger. He found himself, once more, pausing before the house of Mrs. Dorn. Then, as though in answer to his wish, the door flew open and Kitty Murran stood in the shaft of light. Gabriel, still in his painter's apron, stood behind her.

"Oh, no," he heard Kitty Murran say.

"You don't need to come home with me. I'm at home in San Pablo day or night!" So the door closed and she came quickly down through the ruined garden and through the rusted gate, and so out onto the sidewalk. She started a little at the sight of Corcoran but knew him by the manner in which he lifted his hat.

"You haven't been waiting for me all this time," said she. "You *haven't!*"

"Off and on," said Corcoran smoothly. "I don't like to see a girl wandering about through the streets of a wild town like this at night."

She went on beside him with her hands dropped into the pockets of her coat, her face constantly turning toward him so that the starlight glinted over her smile. There was no doubt that she was very keenly flattered by his marked attention and his courtesy.

"That's mighty fine of you," she said, "but — I guess you're not a born Westerner."

"I confess I'm not."

"Well, Easterners never quite understand about it, even if they've been out here for years. But you see, no matter how rough these people may be, or how many crimes the men may have committed, they'll risk their lives, every one of them, to help a woman. If I were to cry out, you'd be amazed to see them come with their guns, ready to kill."

He looked down at her with a faint smile. Of course there was some truth in what she said, but her ardent belief in the goodness of men amused him a little and made him, at the same time, a little sad.

"The poor Dorns!" she sighed. "They are so honest, so enthusiastic, so true to their ideals, but so wretchedly poor. Oh, Mr. Corcoran, men like you can't understand what struggles they pass through. I can tell by your manner of walking and holding your head, even if Willie had never told me a word about you, that you are one of those who do pretty much what they please. Well — the Dorns are people who want to do big, fine things, but they haven't quite the strength. They are people who need help, you know. Poor things! If they could only have an easier chance in life!"

It was so girlishly fine and foolish, all this talk, that it made Corcoran bite his lip to keep from laughing. But he felt, too, that this young crusader was in perilously great need of watching.

She was on again with the subject of the Dorns.

"Her husband hung the weight around their necks. He was one of those strong men who have one weakness. He couldn't resist cards. He was a gambler!"

Corcoran gripped his stick.

"When I think of what gambling does," cried Kitty Murran, "I think it's worse than drunkenness and murder! But if men who throw away what they've earned honestly are bad — think of the people who make gambling a profession! Think of them!"

Corcoran had no desire to think.

"If they were all gathered together in one ship in the middle of the ocean, what a blessing from God to sink that ship and forget every cold-blooded fiend on board it!"

"That's rather hard, Miss Murran. There might be some halfway respectable men aboard."

"How can you say that!"

"Did you ever gamble?"

"No, I thank God!"

"Then you only know —"

"What does one need except eyes and ears to understand?"

"Could you forgive a drunkard?"

"That's disgusting. But then — so much of it begins in just good fellowship. Yes, one could forgive a drunkard, I think. Poor fellows! They injure no one but themselves, after all. But a gambler! Think of stealing out of the pockets of other men."

"Well," said Corcoran, "what are the financiers doing?"

"Can you compare gambling to that?"

"The financiers are playing with the money of other people."

"They make things."

"And sometimes spoil things. However, their main interest is the gamble, isn't it? What will happen? Will the market go up or down? It's the uncertainty that gives the charm."

"Well, I don't admit your argument at all."

"Of course you don't. But consider yourself. You like to teach, don't you?"

"Oh, yes!"

"Why?"

At this, she paused for a long time, with her head raised, not lowered in thought.

"The children are so wonderful," she said softly.

"That's true, I suppose. But isn't the main interest in the new pupils? And in every one of the old ones aren't you saying to yourself: 'How may they turn out? May there be a streak of gold in this one? May that little liar turn into a poet? May that big bully turn into a strong hero? May that quiet little boy some day be a philosopher?' How many possibilities look back at you every morning? Enough force, perhaps, in those young brains, to change history. To conquer nations, or wreck their own. If only you can develop it, with a gambler's luck to —"

She stamped her foot and stopped short.

"After talking like that, how can you end so? Gambling! I'd as soon handle poison."

"Why, you must consider the gambler intimately. You have to get on the inside of anything in order to understand it, don't you think? Suppose yourself a gambler at a table, with the cards in your hands. Here are four other men sitting around the table with you. You never saw them before. They may be clever, they may be stupid. They may be experienced or not. You don't know. They are fighting to take your money. You are fighting to take theirs. The cards are dealt around the table. What have you to go by? A general has the reports of his spies before he fights. You have only what you see. One man looks very grave; perhaps he is looking sober to cover his pleasure. His hand is high. Another is very gay; he smiles and shifts in his chair. Perhaps his hand is high, but he intends to bluff. Those are the tokens that a gambler must go by. Those are his omens. He is not dealing in cards and money, but in minds. A word, a sigh, a lifted eyebrow, a set jaw, a perspiring face, a flush, paleness, restlessness, or a thousand smaller things which one can see in the face, but never put into words — that is the print in the book which he has to read. He may ruin others; he may be himself ruined."

"To hear that, one would think that you admire them!"

"I have known gamblers I admire."

"Really! Well, Mr. Corcoran —" Here she paused and went on a little less passionately: "What of their cheating? Will you try to dignify even that?"

"Perhaps. I have known gamblers who never cheated an honest man."

"But I have heard it said that every gambler has his tricks."

"That may be. But some of them save their tricks for the tricksters."

"You talk very intimately about them."

"I am a professional gambler, Miss Murran!"

At this, she stopped and faced him. "I don't believe it!" cried she.

"God bless your kind heart," said he. "Nevertheless it is true."

"Then — why did you let me say so much?"

"Because I wanted you to commit yourself. I wanted to see how great a handicap I had to — gamble against!"

"What do you mean by that? No, don't answer me!"

She pressed her hands against her face.

"Shall I leave you?" asked Corcoran gently.

"No, no! What a cruel, sharp person you must think me!" Then, as though she wanted to say something but had not the words for it, she rested her hand lightly in the crook of his arm and they walked on together. Not a word was spoken. They avoided the main street and so, by a circuitous route, they came to a little house on the opposite edge of the town, set off behind a hedge and a little garden, a pretty and peaceful place.

"What shall I say to you?" she asked as she stood before him at the gate.

"If you are very kind, that you will let me try to become a friend, Miss Murran."

"Oh," she said, "how terribly one's tongue will gallop. But is it true?" she added, the horror creeping into her voice. "Are you really a gambler?"

"Suppose that I were to tell you that if it seems such an unclean thing to you, I shall cease to be a gambler from this moment?"

There was enough moonlight to show her flush to him.

"Would you do that?"

"I would," said he.

"I cannot take a promise from you," said she.

"I understand, of course." He drew the slender body of the cane through his fingers, waiting.

She said a little haltingly: "I feel that you are doing me a real honor, Mr. Corcoran."

"And embarrassing you, also? You see, Miss Murran, I have come to think a great deal of Willie. I want to make his friends my friends."

She drew a great breath of relief, feeling all sentimentality brushed from the air. Then: "I *am* going to take that promise, Mr. Corcoran."

They shook hands upon it. "With all my heart," said he. "After all, it was a rotten business, you know."

CHAPTER 16

He went back to the hotel slowly, thinking over everything carefully. Now and then his face grew hot. He felt that he had done a great deal upon the basis of so meager an acquaintance. And yet, remembering her, and her frankness, and her fine, quiet voice, and the wealth of her enthusiasm, he lost his embarrassment. As for giving up the gambling, he told himself that it was nothing. To gain even the first step in her friendship was a far greater thing. Having gained that step perhaps he could go on and on to a larger thing. He stopped and made a gesture of defiance at the stars. Let the man step forth who was to challenge him in this duel!

When he reached the hotel, he saw that the rose he had placed in his buttonhole was sadly withered. He plucked it out, but still held it in his hand as he went through the lobby. There were few in it. The majority were away finding amusement, and one could hear what they had found. It blew faintly through the open door of the hotel — a strange murmur made up of light, high voices of women and deep, strong voices of men, all running up the scale and down again.

There were men enough in the lobby, however, to grace his entrance with their attention. They did not even have to call the attention of one another by whispering his name. He was known by this time. All conversation stopped. And their glances attended him as he went up the stairs.

He was humming when he opened the door of his room. He was still humming when he turned from lighting his lamp and saw young Willie Kern seated calmly in the big chair before the window puffing at a cigarette whose smoke was drawn swiftly into the open night.

"Hello," said Willie.

"Hello," said Corcoran. "I see that you have a black eye."

"I bumped agin' a tree in the dark," said Willie, yawning deliberately.

"That's the trouble with the night," said Corcoran. "It often gets a man into trouble." And he winked.

"Sure," said Willie, and winked back.

"I'm afraid," said Corcoran, "that others have run into trees this evening."

"Four of 'em," said Willie. "Dog-goned if four of 'em didn't run into trees and get so blind that they kept on bumpin'. You'd be surprised to see the way they look."

"No doubt," grinned Corcoran.

"Every one of 'em had to holler for help," said Willie.

"I hope you were by to lend a hand," said Corcoran.

"I done what I could," said Willie, and looked down at the skinned knuckles of his right fist. "You done 'em brown in Ted Rankin's didn't you!" His eyes were on fire with enthusiasm.

"Were you there?"

"Sure."

"I didn't see you."

"There was a knot hole right behind Cracken's table."

"Ah," said Corcoran. "What happened after I left?"

"Mr. Roland, he shoved the money into a sack and said that he'd keep it till the thing was settled. Ain't he a *man?*"

"He is."

"Cracken was sort of nervous. He sneaked away through the crowd. I knew he was goin' back to the office to see Rankin. I went along — outside. They wasn't no cracks in the wall there in the office, but I could listen. It's fair to listen to crooks, ain't it?"

"Why," said Corcoran, "perhaps it is."

"Rankin was sort of excited. Did you ever hear him cuss?"

"No."

"I knowed a gent that used to drive mules up to Comanche Mountain. He had a string of sixteen. They was all ornery critters. Balkin' in the middle of a hill was their idea of a good game. Dog-goned if he didn't have a separate line of cussing for every one of them mules. He was the outbeatin'est gent at swearin' that ever I heard. But last night Rankin, take him by and large, he laid over anything that mule driver ever done in the way of cussin'. When he got through: 'You're yaller!' says he.

"The voice of Cracken answers up right pronto: 'I'll tear your heart out, you fat rat, if you say that ag'in!'

" 'What're you goin' to do about meetin' Corcoran?' says Rankin.

" 'That ain't my party,' said Cracken. 'I said that I'd stop that game, and I done it. I'll take my coin now, Rankin.'

" 'What coin?' says Rankin.

" 'That's too thin,' yells Cracken. 'About eight thousand berries is all I want.'

" 'Eight thousand for what?' says Rankin.

" 'For stoppin' the game.'

" 'For stoppin' Corcoran,' said Rankin. 'You ain't stopped him. You just put him off. He'll be back here raisin' the devil with my bank account to-morrow. I ain't got a dealer that's man enough to stand up to him.'

" 'You've talked enough,' says Cracken. 'This here is the right time for payin'. You can talk later on.'

" 'Cracken,' says he, gettin' sort of persuasive, 'you ain't goin' to try to trim me? After the way I've lost today?'

" 'Eight thousand is all the tune I'm talkin',' says Cracken. 'I'll have it now — pronto, right quick in my hand. Start in countin' it out!'

" 'All right,' says Rankin. 'If you're goin' to force my hand, you got to have it. Come in, boys.'

"I dunno what happened then, but I guess maybe that three or four gents come in through the door lookin' ready for trouble. Anyways, pretty soon Cracken pipes up mighty soft and says: 'Don't be a fool, Rankin. Can't you take a joke?'

" 'Sure,' says Rankin, 'but I thought you couldn't. All right, boys.'

"They tramped out ag'in. Then Rankin says: 'Well, Cracken, you see how it is. I can't afford to throw eight thousand away for nothin'.'

" 'Sure,' says Cracken. 'I'm willin' to compromise.'

" 'I always knowed that you had sense,' says Rankin. 'But they's only one way to run this here game.'

" 'What's that?' says Cracken, talkin' pretty thick.

" 'My way,' says Rankin.

"They wasn't nothin' said for a while, but I could hear big Cracken walkin' up and down slow and steady makin' the floor creak underneath him. After a while he says: 'When the pack is stacked, a gent is a fool that sits in at a game, if he knows. Well, Rankin, just now you got the say. What is it?'

" 'It's just this, old son. You've had the taste of that eight thousand.'

" 'I dunno what you call a taste,' says Cracken.

" 'Does this look like something to you?' says Rankin.

" 'Well — that *is* a taste. Go on, Rankin. You always been pretty open-handed. I don't mind sayin' that I'd trust you more'n I'd trust any other man I know.'

" 'The devil,' says Rankin. 'You've showed how much you'd trust me. But I ain't talkin' about trust. I'm talkin' about the facts. I need you, and you need the money I can pay you. Is that right?'

" 'That's one way of puttin' it.'

" 'Well, Cracken, we got to get rid of this here Corcoran. He's got the number of our joint. He'll never stop until he has us on the run. He'll ruin me, old-timer.'

" 'No doubt about that.'

" 'Then I say that we got to take another crack at him.'

" 'Meanin' me?'

" 'That's it.'

" 'Not me, Rankin. That gent is bad medicine. I don't want no part of his game.'

" 'Cracken,' says he, 'you might as well figure that you'll have to meet up with him some day.'

" 'How come?'

" 'Ain't you called him a crook?'

" 'My good heavens,' says Cracken, 'I must be crazy. I'd near forgot all about that!'

" 'It ain't a thing to forget, though.'

" 'As far as I'm concerned, I ain't interested in San Pablo no more. I'll take a trip.'

" 'You run out on Corcoran,' says Rankin, spattin' his hands together, 'and your name is Dennis all over the mountains. Nobody but a Chinaman will be seen talkin' to you. Besides no matter how fast or how far you run, d'you think that you could ever get away from Corcoran? He's a greyhound, that gent. And he don't never forget nothin' nor forgive nothin'. Now, Cracken, you sit tight and listen to what I got to say!'

"Right then was when I started in listenin' the hardest, but I didn't hear nothin'. They was talkin' in whispers. Every once in a while I could hear Cracken grunt. Then Rankin would start in again, the first word loud and the rest all soft. They talked on for quite a spell. I dunno what they was sayin', but it wasn't nothin' that meant any good for you, I guess."

"I guess not," agreed Corcoran. "But thank you for what you found out, Willie."

"That's nothing," said Willie. "I guess you don't aim to stay on around San Pablo?"

"Why not?"

"Why not? Well, Mr. Corcoran, this here Rankin — you know him, don't you?"

"A little."

"Then you know that he's got about a hundred gents in San Pablo that would do anything he wants 'em to do. He just about runs the town. He's got men — why, they wouldn't think nothin' of runnin' a knife into your back while you was asleep!"

"I'll think it over," said Corcoran. "But in the meantime this seems a very interesting town to me. What became of Miss Murran, Willie?"

The boy yawned again. "There ain't no use of me botherin' my head about her no more," said he.

"Why not?"

"Her man has come back to town," said Willie.

The blood of Corcoran ran like ice through his body. "Her man?" he echoed feebly and faintly.

"Sure, her man."

"You mean, some one she is married to?"

"The same thing. Somebody that she's engaged to marry. And her kind of a woman — they do what they say they'll do. Ain't that right?"

"I suppose it is," said Corcoran huskily. "Engaged to be married." He went hastily to his carryall and extracted from it a flask from which he took a generous drag. "What about this fellow?" he asked, with his back turned.

"It's him that she come West with."

"What?"

"She was away visitin'. Away back in the East. When she came back she brought her man along with her. He went out workin'

164

through the mines, you see; that was where he was goin' to invest his money."

"He's rich, then?" said Corcoran gloomily.

"Sure. He dunno how much money he's got, I guess. Heaps of it!"

"But he lets her teach school?"

"I guess that's her way. Maybe he's got to like her country before he can have her."

"What's his name?" asked Corcoran sharply.

"It couldn't be but one man, Mr. Corcoran. It's that Big Roland."

CHAPTER 17

Corcoran leaned over and busied himself dusting imaginary sand from the cuff of his trouser leg for a moment before he was able to look up, sure of himself and confident that his face would not betray him.

"He's a pretty fine fellow, I suppose," said Corcoran.

"He thought he knowed you," said Willie Kern.

"He mistook me for another man. Yes."

"He thought you was the same as a football player that he used to know."

"That was it, I believe."

"How could a gent like you play football, bein' so skinny?"

"I told you that he had made a mistake."

"You don't weigh much more'n a hundred and fifty — with your clothes on, Mr. Corcoran!"

"Hardly that. No, Roland was absurd about the football."

Willie Kern dropped his chin upon his fist

and studied the man with a thoughtful scowl. "They's been some light ones, though," he remarked. "They was Ingram that used to play quarter on —"

"What do you know about football, son?"

"Me? I've read all about it. Right back to the days of the old-timers. That Raymond, he weighed in around a hundred and forty. He played quarter, and used to smash the line, dog-goned if he didn't."

"He was a great player," said Corcoran.

"Maybe you knowed him?" snapped out the boy quickly.

"I've heard of him," said Corcoran biting his lip as he saw how close he had come to betraying himself.

"Then that gent Chambers — he played quarter and half. He could do pretty near anything. He didn't weigh no more. There was the greatest of 'em all — that Burlington. Ever hear of him?"

Corcoran coughed behind his hand. "I don't think so," he said.

"He hardly weighed a hundred and forty. He played end and nobody got around him for two seasons. Think of that."

"He was lucky, then."

"Lucky? Him? Nope. They used to call him the mind reader. He always knowed where the ball was goin', and he always got in the way. He could kick, too. Once he dropped her over from the fifty-two-yard line. Think of that!"

It seemed to Corcoran that he felt again the heavy impact of the ball against his toe — that he saw it rise high — that he saw it float like a dangling balloon aloft — that once more it was dropping toward the cross bar — that fifty thousand people sat breathless to watch — that it wafted at last between the posts and over the bar!

"A long kick," he managed to say.

"And sixty yards was nothin' with his puntin'. That was Burlington! But take him on the line and they wasn't nobody could handle him. He went through like he was greased lightning. Every time he tackled a gent, time out was called! That was Burlington! They'll never have another like him! Well, Mr. Corcoran, dog-gone if Burlington was any bigger than you when he —"

A light hand tapped at the door.

"I'll be goin'," said the boy hastily, and instantly vanished through the window. Corcoran heard the bare feet scuff on the roof below; then he opened the door and admitted none other than Gabriel Dorn.

The painter stood before him, stroking his little black mustache and grinning.

"Pardon a stranger for troubling you,"

said he. "But I have business with you, Mr. Corcoran. My name is Gabriel Dorn."

He was waved to a chair by Corcoran, who lingered a moment closing the door in order that some of the violent distaste which he felt for the man might disappear from his eyes. He turned at last to find Dorn comfortably ensconced in the big chair by the window, where Willie Kern had been sitting the moment before.

"All of San Pablo is buzzing your name," said the painter.

"San Pablo is very kind," said Corcoran grimly.

"Ah? Perhaps rather curious than kind," returned Dorn. "But for my part, I have felt moved to do you a service, Mr. Corcoran."

The gambler bowed. He could not look at the other without having his gorge rise.

"In short, sir, I have brought you a warning!" He said it solemnly, and Corcoran nodded.

"This is very good of you," he said. "One has enemies, of course."

"The man of whom I speak," said Dorn, "is not your enemy as yet."

"But he is about to become one?"

"I hope not."

"What do you mean?" This with a touch of impatience.

"I mean that it rests with you. I am speaking of the most formidable man in San Pablo, Mr. Corcoran — a strong man, a rich man, and a fighter by instinct! But you guess?"

"I have not the slightest idea in the world, I assure you."

"Consider again. You have met him face to face this very evening, I know!"

"You seem to have seen rather more of me than I have seen of you, Mr. Dorn."

Dorn flushed. "One cannot help using one's eyes. And in this matter, I could not help feeling that it was my duty."

"Quite so. Your duty, by all means. In the first place, let's have the name of the man."

"I assure you, Mr. Corcoran, I run considerable risk in mixing into his business."

"I feel your generosity very keenly."

"In short, sir, the name of the man is no other than Henry Pertwee Roland!"

With this master stroke, he leaned back in his chair and regarded Corcoran with an air of malicious triumph, a spot of color glowing in the center of either cheek. Corcoran, in fact, was strongly startled. He could not believe his ears at first, so he stood with his feet braced, staring down at the thin face of the artist.

"Tell me how under heaven this could be!" he demanded.

"What is the matter about which Mr. Roland is most touchy? You will guess at once! It is the lady to whom he is engaged in marriage!"

A drunken cow-puncher raced his horse down the main street to San Pablo, his wild song rushing through the open window of Corcoran's room; then in a trice the song was gone and the hoofbeats, muffled in the thick dust, drummed far away.

"What in relation to Miss Murran," he asked, "could bring the anger of Roland on me?"

"In short, sir, you were seen with her."

"What the devil does that —"

"Mr. Roland is an extraordinarily jealous man, sir."

There was no doubt of that. Even in a rival university, Corcoran could remember hearing tales of the immense pride and fierce passions of Roland.

"I have met Miss Murran and escorted her to her home. What is there in that worthy of being talked about?"

"Sir, you do not know Mr. Roland. Consider this: That San Pablo is filled with strong fellows and rough fellows who all have an eye for a pretty girl, but rough and strong as they are, not one of them has ever dared to take a moment of Miss Murran's time since Roland appeared in her life. That is to say, Sharkness was the last. He thought that the game was open until the marriage ceremony was actually performed; Roland convinced him that he was wrong, and though he paid the hospital bill afterward, Sharkness has been a wreck of a man ever since. He was a wild fellow, too, that Sharkness. He's hardly better than half alive now!"

"Who has carried this tale to Roland about me?"

"No one — as yet!"

"Who is apt to do so?"

"A man who is wavering between his sense of duty and his — sense of humanity, sir."

"In short — yourself!"

"Mr. Corcoran, I believe that I may as well be frank. Yes, it is I!"

"What has brought you here, sir?"

Before the sternness of Corcoran, Dorn did not so much as wince. He was as one who holds in his hand a trump card of invincible strength.

"A desire to give you some good advice, Mr. Corcoran."

"I am buried in obligation to you, Mr. Dorn."

"Not at all! I have no doubt that you will be able to arrange the matter to the entire satisfaction of both of us."

"Yours and mine?"

"Of course. I realize that you have a formidable reputation as a fighting man, sir. I also realize that you are not a fool and that you will not stake that reputation against the hands of a lion like Henry Roland."

"Perhaps I shall not. Then you will tell me, Mr. Dorn, what arrangement I can make to keep you from carrying this news to Roland?"

"Oh," said Dorn, waving an airy hand and then helping himself from the gold cigarette case of his host, "as to the terms, I leave them entirely to you."

"You want money, then?"

"I am a wretchedly poor man, sir," answered Dorn through a cloud of smoke.

His effrontery and shamelessness abashed Corcoran, in spite of all of his experience with strange men in strange places.

"Well, then, name the terms, Mr. Dorn."

Dorn cleared his throat, and looking up to the ceiling, he considered the matter at his genial ease.

"One must keep in mind the fact that

Roland is a killer — a very devilish fighter, Mr. Corcoran."

"We must never forget that, of course."

"Just so! Then we come to the fact that this matter is the thing that is nearest to his heart. We come to the understanding that he might be extraordinarily excited if he were to know that the lady of his heart was escorted to her home this evening by one who — who might be scandalously called merely a gambler."

The angry veins stood purple across the forehead of Corcoran. "There are other things," he said. "You must remember that Mr. Roland may hear of the great interest which the lady takes in you and your mother, my friend."

"Tush," said the blackmailer, "that is a mere nothing. I assure you that I have taken care never to be a minute alone with her. Scandal can raise not the slightest whisper against me! No, no — besides, he knows and sympathizes with her kind interest in my art!"

There was a faint exclamation from Corcoran, but the other went blindly on, unheeding.

"Taking all of these matters into your consideration, may we not say that, to a person like you, Mr. Corcoran, who takes in ten thousand dollars in a single profitable evening — and considering also the greatness of the danger from which you are delivered — may we not say that — twenty-five hundred dollars would not be too much? May we not call that a very cheap price?"

"Very!" murmured Corcoran, breathing hard. "I confess that I hold my life at a higher price."

"By all means. I do not wish to be grasping. Not at all!"

"Concerning yourself," said Corcoran suddenly, "is it not strange that Miss Murran has never seen the truth about you?"

"I don't understand, sir."

"How can she have avoided noticing that you and Mrs. Dorn are a pair of worthless adventurers — drunken, shaming, scoundrelly farces! How can she have avoided noticing these things? For, after all, she is a person of intelligence, you know."

Mr. Dorn blinked at his host for a moment. An instant before, he had been mentally thumbing a thick sheaf of bank notes. His mother would not be bothered by them or the spending of them. He would go away to the East and the South as fast as the trains could bear him. He would equip himself with fine feathers. He would make of himself the figure of a man which he felt was his right.

These pleasant visions had been unrolling before the mind's eye of Dorn. Now he saw his happy dream torn asunder with a brutal violence. The man whom he felt he had browbeaten to the verge of trembling submission was staring at him now with something wolfish in his eyes that made strange sensations pass quivering through the body of Mr. Dorn.

"Mr. Corcoran," he said, "if we cannot agree —" His trembling voice could master no further words.

"We can agree," said Corcoran coldly, "to see no more of one another. There is the door, Mr. Dorn."

Mr. Gabriel Dorn glided swiftly to it.

"Your hat," said Corcoran.

And, as the door opened and he clapped the hat upon the head of his departing guest, he saw before him the sheer downward pitch of the stairs dropping into the gloom of the next landing. The temptation formed irresistibly in the brain of Corcoran. If a man can drop kick a football fifty-two yards, how far can he kick —

Mr. Dorn with a frightened yell felt himself impelled upward and forward with terrific violence. He made a frantic clutch at the banister, missed it, and hurtled head foremost into view at the landing. The fat man dodged in the nick of time, and Mr. Dorn tumbled head over heels out of sight.

CHAPTER 18

Corcoran, however, did not smile. He was considering all the grave possibilities which might arise out of this affair. For Dorn, like a beaten cur, was almost certain to go whining to big Henry Roland with some garbled account of what had passed between him and the gambler and of what had passed between the gambler and the girl. And if Roland were once thoroughly aroused, what might not the results be?

These thoughts made him stand for a moment at the entrance to his room, and before he had an opportunity to close the door, a fat man rose perspiring and puffing before him in the person of one no less distinguished than Mr. Theodore Rankin, who now thrust forth a fat, moist hand to be shaken by Corcoran. He bustled on into the room and stood gazing with a rather pale, uneasy smile about him.

"Flowers, dog-gone me!" exclaimed Mr. Rankin. "Why, Mr. Corcoran, you got this here room all fixed up fine as a fiddle, eh? Some folks know how to make the most of things."

At this rather feeble attempt to propitiate his host, the host himself smiled and then invited the proprietor of the gaming house to be seated.

Mr. Rankin reposed his fat self upon the very edge of a straight chair with his hat in one hand and both his pudgy palms pressed strongly upon his knees. He gave an impression of one about to start up and race for the door at the first sign of danger.

"Was that Gabriel Dorn that I seen tryin' to turn himself into a night hawk and fly?" asked the fat man.

"He tripped at the head of the stairs," said Corcoran.

The other grinned broadly. This was the sort of jest at which he felt himself at home.

"Well," he said, "I've heard of gents stumblin' like that. Dog-goned if I didn't think that he was goin' to hit me and knock a hole in me."

He went on genially, lowering his voice a little and glancing toward the window: "I guess there ain't nobody in hearing of us, Mr. Corcoran?"

Corcoran went to the window and looked out. He saw half of the wide curve of the heavens, dotted with stars, and a wind laden with the fragrance of the mountain evergreens blew gently in to him. San Pablo was quieting down little by little. Far off, the music in the dance hall was breathing, but the street itself was still. The pleasure hunters had found their appropriate places and were content.

"There is no one in hearing," he said, turning back to his guest.

"Good!" said the gambler, and rubbed his thick soft hands nervously together. "That makes it better. I got something to talk about to you, Corcoran, that don't need to be listened in on by nobody else." He leaned far forward in the chair and raised an admonitory forefinger for silence and attention. "What I'm goin' to say has to do with your life, Corcoran!" He added in surprise and some anger: "It ain't no laughin' matter, Mr. Corcoran.

The smile of Corcoran had been at the thought of how the last man who brought a warning to him had made his exit that night just as Rankin entered.

"Of course not," said Corcoran. "As a matter of fact, I was thinking of another matter. Tell me what's up?"

"It's Cracken. Dog-goned if he ain't gone wild!"

"About what, Rankin? Because he knows that he lied when he said that he saw me cheat in that last deal?"

"Maybe that's it," admitted the other with wonderful frankness, as though he had nothing intimately to do with the affair. "You know how some of these here gents are!"

"Of course," admitted Corcoran.

"But Cracken says now that it's either him or you. Dog-goned if I don't think that he'd run out on the fight, but he figures that you'd never rest till you fought it out with him. You'd trail him down somewheres, he says."

"Perhaps."

"So he's got his back to the wall. Ever see a cornered rat fight, Corcoran?"

"No."

"I turned loose a rattler in a cage again' a big gray rat, once. They sure battled. The rat was scared mighty near to death when he heard the rattle buzz. And the snake got all ready to fix himself a nice little dinner. He coiled himself up and began wavin' his head back and forth to get a chance to wallop that rat and swaller it. If they'd been an open place, the rat would of just turned to run and got gobbled. But he seen that he couldn't get away, so he started fightin'. He dodged around the rattler like a streak of dust in a high wind. He sunk them needle teeth of his into that old snake about a hundred times.

"And the rattler fanged him a couple of times, too. But dog-goned me if that rat would die for a long time. Finally he got a grip on the back of that rattler's head and he hung on there like a bulldog till he dropped off and died from the poison. The snake wasn't none too lively, neither. By the next mornin', it was dead, too."

"You mean," said Corcoran at the conclusion of this stirring narrative, "that Cracken would fight like that?"

"He sure would."

"He'll have his opportunity tomorrow at noon."

"Wait a minute, Corcoran. Cracken has got to stay. He wouldn't have no reputation left if he didn't turn up to face you, would he?"

"No more than I would have if I failed to face him."

"That's where you're wrong, old son. A reputation like yours ain't spoiled in a minute by any one thing."

Corcoran sat down and locked his hands around his lean knees.

"In short," he said, "what is it all about?

What do you want me to do, Rankin?"

The other spatted his fat hands together. "I want you to get out of town!" he said sharply.

"Yes?"

"Not for nothin' — I ain't a fool. I'll pay your way. First place, I don't like to see a fine young gent like you get all shot up."

Corcoran raised his hand with a smile of protest and Rankin hurried on, coloring a little. "Besides, what is there for you to gain?"

"About seventy-five hundred and a chance to teach a ruffian some necessary manners. That's enough, I take it, to make the fight worth while."

"Manners? What good would manners be with poor old Cracken? About the money — you don't have to worry. It's comin' to you —"

"When Roland and the others see me win, they'll hand it over, you mean?"

For answer, Rankin opened his coat, and keeping his glance fixed upon the gambler, to read his face, he drew forth a bulging wallet. It flopped open in his hand of its own tension. There was revealed within each side of the wallet a dense mass of bills packed together as thick and as closely as the pressed leaves of a volume. But

Corcoran regarded this spectacle without a murmur of comment — without a change of expression. And the gambler sighed in despair. When a man cannot be reached by money, what can reach him? Nevertheless, he decided to make his attempt.

"I brought some cash along," he said, "figurin' that I could wipe out one of the causes for you stayin'. I brung along all that you won the other night, and a mite more, Corcoran just a mite more!"

His ferret-bright eyes worked at the face of Corcoran eagerly, hoping against hope, as it were, and not finding what he wished for.

"It won't do, Rankin," said Corcoran quietly. "It won't do at all, I tell you. I stay right here in San Pablo until I'm ready to leave. Money won't buy me." He even laughed, adding: "This will save you time and it will save me embarrassment, I hope. You can't bribe me to go, Rankin."

He stood up, and Rankin, taking the hint, rose also.

"That ain't no friendly way of talkin', Corcoran," he said grimly.

"I'm not your enemy, Rankin," said the gambler without emotion, "unless you wish to treat me as one. But if you do —" He snapped his thin fingers in the air above his head.

"It ain't me," said Rankin. "But you know what'll come of you when all this here gets out? You know what Mike Nolan will be ready for?"

"What?" asked Corcoran.

"He'll be standin' by to shoot down the first gent that pulls a gun."

Corcoran shook his head. "I don't think," he said, "that Mike Nolan cares a whit what comes of Cracken or of me. If we were to butcher one another, he would be that much happier. He would have two difficulties brushed out of his path — two centers of trouble removed. It would be a case of poison fighting poison, so far as the sheriff is concerned. No, I don't think that he'll interfere."

"They say," said Rankin sneeringly, his pretense of friendliness rapidly disappearing, "that you read the minds of folks."

"Sometimes I try. Usually, however, I find that it is not worth while."

The worthy Rankin was at least adroit enough to feel the sting of this remark. He favored Corcoran with a black scowl and made for the door. There he paused for an instant with his hand upon the knob, but thinking better of the vindictive words which rose to the tip of his tongue, he jerked the door open and thudded his way down the stairs. He had only one way of showing his contempt for Corcoran, and that was by failing to close the door behind him as he disappeared into the gloom of the stairway.

CHAPTER 19

There was gloom in the face of Corcoran as he closed the door, and he began to walk softly up and down the room to order his thoughts. His ebony cane was the companion on such occasions. Sometimes he spun it between his fingers. Sometimes he drew it delicately through his hands. Sometimes he held it forth before him and admired its taper straightness with the high light running down its length like a rapier. It was suggestive of Corcoran, that slight walking stick. It had his suppleness, his illusive strength. But while his hands and his eyes were busy with it, his thoughts were far away.

He could see, now that he had betrayed himself into an entirely false position. For the sake of a girl who was engaged to another man — a man, too, far worthier of her than was Corcoran — he had forsworn his delight and his staff of life, gambling. For her sake, too, he had given up his gun and taken to peaceful ways. But as he reviewed the situation, he could not help but smile at the beautiful completeness of his folly. Before to-morrow night he would be either a dead man in a street brawl, or else the destroyer of another life. In either case, he could guess clearly enough what would go on in the mind of the girl concerning him. If his frank confession had disarmed half of her scorn of him as a gambler, perhaps it was only for the moment, and reflection would make her detest him.

But, no matter what she thought or felt, at noon of the morrow, he would have to face Joe Cracken, gun in hand. He paused to rearrange his necktie before the mirror. He settled his hat upon his head. He selected another rose from the bouquet near the window which was filling the room with the peppery sweetness of its fragrance. Then, cane in hand, he went forth into the street.

He met an old acquaintance before he had gone forth twenty paces down the sidewalk. Skinny Montague, though he might not have had good fortune at the gaming tables, was at least sure of some return for his day's work. He had in tow a huge, lumbering fellow from the mines, the bandanna loosened at his throat, his shirt opened to take the coolness of the evening, his sombrero atilt on the back of his head, and his walk an uncertain, fumbling stagger of drunkenness. Plainly he had sat at the elbow of moonshine whiskey as a boon companion that night. Plainly, also, his money belt was loaded. One can tell prosperity in a miner drunk or sober, wet or dry. It exudes from them like radiance from a jewel or perfume from a flower. They looked about them with a peculiar hunger of the eyes which bespeaks the mighty will to spend.

Skinny Montague supported this looming hulk with difficulty. But though he perspired, he stuck to his work. He reminded Corcoran of a little tug laboring into port with a great derelict as a prize. Certainly he knew that his work would not be without its reward. He greeted Corcoran with a grin and a wink as the latter went by. And Corcoran paused.

"I am going to call on your friend in the morning," said he.

"You are?" said Skinny. "Well, pal, I dunno that it'll be worth your while."

"I think it will."

"Look here," grunted Montague. "What's the meaning of all that?"

"I have something to ask your friend, yonder."

"Frien'?" droned the drunkard. "Tha's me. I'm ev'rybody's frien'. Say, Skinny —

gimme 'nother drink, will you?"

"What you got to ask him?" snapped Skinny.

"How his accounts stand," said Corcoran.

"He won't find no way of puttin' 'em right," said Skinny.

"I think he will," said Corcoran.

"You mean you'll butt into this? Ain't you had your fun? D'you have to spoil mine?"

"Skinny," said Corcoran, "be a man. If you play rat, I'll set a trap and catch you. Let that poor fellow's pocketbook alone."

"Bah!" snarled out Skinny, shaking with wrath. "You're playin' bully, Corcoran. Luck has spoiled your head." He ducked away from his burden. "Let him take care of his fool self, then!" growled out Skinny, and disappeared around the corner of the building.

The drunkard staggered to leeward like a ship without headway struck by a gale; but Corcoran took him instantly in charge. In ten minutes he had him safely asleep in a room at the hotel, which was already crowded.

"Friends," said the gambler to them, "this is a partner of mine. I hope he'll have good luck here!"

They grinned broadly at him. There was

no doubting his meaning, and he left the place with the assurance that the big, helpless miner would go untouched in safety and pocketbook. Unless, of course, there were in San Pablo, those who could afford to make light of Corcoran and the magic of his gun, which was a thing that he had cause to doubt.

He returned to the street and went straight to the house of the sheriff. The shades of the front room were raised, and there was revealed a picture of domestic bliss — Mrs. Sheriff Nolan rocking in a corner chair with a lap full of sewing, and the sheriff himself in shirt sleeves rolled up high enough to expose his red-flannel underwear. A newspaper hardly more than a fortnight old was expanded before him, and his pipe, the stem of which had been chewed away and rebitted until it fairly singed his mustaches, gripped firmly in the corner of his mouth.

"I see they been gettin' after them land grafters, M'ria."

"Well, well, Mike!"

And she went on humming her song softly, softly, and working an enormous patch upon the seat of a diminutive pair of trousers.

"That there Darnley, looks like he took a

bride, right enough."

"How folks do carry on, Mike!"

And her soft humming began again, only two phrases of a song heard in her girlhood, the source forgotten, a bit of mental driftwood cast ashore and saved from oblivion, a tuneless line of music now grown a part of her subconscious self, a ceaseless drone that had lightened the labors of fifteen years of housewifery. It was to the sheriff like the sound of machinery to the mill owner — like the noise of the sea to the sailor in the forecastle. Without it a great void would have been struck into his very heart and his soul, but he would never have known what he missed.

Corcoran, standing beside the door, saw, and heard, and understood. He had seen such family groups before, of course, but he had always felt when he looked at them, like a passenger on an overland express when it whips through the outskirts of a lonely prairie town, sunburned, wind-battered, now drenched with cold gray rain. How do people live there? What do they do? Where are their souls? What are the sunsets and the sunrises of their lives?

Such had been the thoughts of Corcoran when he had looked upon such scenes in the past. But this night as he watched and listened it seemed to Corcoran that these people were truly living and that his own life was filled with ghosts only — a ghost among ghosts — all ruin, all sorrow, all endless hopelessness.

Then he tapped on the door. The sheriff came with one hand resting upon his broad hip just above where the gun nestled in the worn leather holster. He cocked his glasses upon his forehead and stood helplessly in the doorway. What a crowning wonder it was that he had not been ten times murdered by his many enemies!

"There is a strength in goodness," said Corcoran to himself, and turned that phrase in his mind like a great discovery.

"It's Corcoran," he said.

"Dog-gone me!" said the sheriff. "I been tellin' M'ria about you. Come in, boy. She'll be right glad to see you. Dog-goned if you didn't come out of Rankin's pretty slick! No gun — and Cracken to deal with!"

"I've come to tell you a new chapter," said Corcoran. "I've come to tell you that I have to take that gun of mine back."

"You ain't meanin' that, Corcoran!"

"I have to have it."

"You swear off gun play this evenin'; you take back your gun to-night." He sighed, and from the holster behind his left hip he took out a revolver and passed it slowly to Corcoran. "It's sure a jim-dandy beauty," he said to Corcoran. "It's got a feel and a hang to it, that gun has. Where you ever pick it up?"

"In a way," said Corcoran, "you might say I inherited it."

"What way d'you mean?"

"Simply that I got it after the death of the man who used to wear it."

The sheriff chuckled. He was pleased by such jesting as this. He could appreciate raw words and bludgeon strokes of wit.

"So," he said, watching Corcoran receive the weapon and fondle it a moment before he put it away in his clothes with a swift and oiled deftness of movement, "so, old-timer, you're on the warpath again? Are you goin' to have me chasin' after you before mornin' for some dog-gone killin'?"

His frankness and curiosity made Corcoran smile. "I hope not," he answered.

"How old are you?" asked Nolan suddenly.

"Thirty."

"And what?"

"Exactly that."

"Only thirty? Why, man, when I was your age, nobody knowed me ten miles away from the range where I was daubin' ropes and huntin' screw worms. Why, Corcoran, it was two year after that before M'ria said she'd wear my name for the sake of bringin' me kids and naggin' me about 'em. I wasn't nothin', at that age, and look at the man you are!"

He came a little farther into the doorway and shaded his eyes with his hand as though that would help him to make out the greatness of the younger man. He added: "Come in, son. I want M'ria to meet up with you."

"No," said Corcoran bluntly. "I'm not worthy of it!" And he went off hastily. Not once did he swing his cane on the way back to the hotel.

CHAPTER 20

It was at this time that Roland and Kitty Murran sat in the garden in front of her boarding house with the cool of the night about them. He was looking down, thinking, planning, and his voice made a deep rumble which seldom paused, as he sketched their future. She followed him half dreamily, with her head pillowed in one arm which she had thrown over the back of her chair, and her eyes raised to the stars where the burly shoulders of Comanche Mountain thrust up into the sky half unreal in the darkness, like a mountain of clouds. So that sometimes she half thought she saw the glimmer of a star midway in the mass; or was it merely a big camp fire whose flames leaped sometimes in the wind and sometimes died away?

"Would that make you happy?"

Suddenly she knew that he had asked the same question three times together.

"Yes," she said hastily.

Roland stirred and then stood up. He

went to the gate and paused there: then he came back and sat down again. She knew that he was very angry. She was a little alarmed, but to her surprise she found that the alarm was not altogether unpleasant.

She said by way of apology: "I was thinking of something."

"Not what I was talking about."

"Forgive me, Henry."

"Oh, of course."

His silence was a sufficient voice for his displeasure.

"Sometimes, it seems to me," he said, "that this West you wanted to see, and which I was so eager to come to, has merely served to make a breech between us."

A denial formed politely on her lips. But she was lazy of mind this evening, and instead she spoke the truth.

"Do you think that? Why?"

"You have had the same feeling?" he asked sharply.

"No, no!"

He said with a certain eagerness: "I've liked it immensely out here. And I've had luck. It's been everything that I imagined, the land and the people. Just as you said to me in New York, I've felt since I came here that I was made for this part of my country. Everything has been as I hoped it might be

— except you, Kitty."

"I'm terribly sorry."

Something like a groan formed in the throat of Roland. "It doesn't make a great difference, it seems to you. Isn't that true?"

"Will you let me be frank?"

"Of course."

The alarm in his voice hurt her and roused a sudden pity. So she stretched out her hand and let it rest lightly on his arm. Apparently he understood. For he allowed the hand to remain there without making any response.

"Well," said she, closing her eyes, but still unable to shut out her thought, "I'm half drowsy to-night. It's hard for me to listen and — put two and two together."

He was instantly repentant. "Poor old dear," said Henry Roland. "You're tired out. What a fool I am to drive you on to talk when you're so tired!"

"Not that — only —"

A silence began, and as it grew, she roused from her languor, for here was something new between them.

"Do you know," said he at last, "that I am gradually beginning to understand the whole affair?"

"What affair, Henry?"

"Between you and me."

"What about it, then?"

"When you first saw me, I was wasting time."

"Outrageously."

"And you wanted to put me to some sort of use. You said to yourself that a fellow with an average good head and a strong brute of a body ought to be doing something better than conditioning hunters. So you began to talk to me about the West. I grew interested. Ten per cent in the country; ninety per cent in you, of course. And as you saw me waking up, you took a pride in me. I thought it was love; it wasn't."

"Henry!"

"Let's be honest. You were mistaken, too. You didn't know. I don't suppose you'd ever cared much for any man, and when you became interested in me, you thought that interest was the real thing, you know. But it isn't. There's something more. I've always felt it. Tonight I know. I think," he went on reverently, "that I love you as no woman was ever loved before. But you, Kate, how do you care for me? Where is the fire? Where is the music and the poetry of real loving?"

He waited for a moment; perhaps he was waiting for her denial, and she tried to utter one, but what he said had filled her mind too full for speech. She was taking up all his ideas and rushing them forward to logical conclusions which she shrank from as she approached them. So, bitterly, he forged ahead again with his analysis.

"Take it all in all, Kate, I represent an investment of your personal attention in a man. You see the investment giving you some return. Arid ground has been made to produce. But when you think of building a home on that ground, you are not particularly enthusiastic."

"But I am, Henry — and —"

"If I ask you to name a day for the marriage, you always turn from that, you know."

"I wonder why?" said she softly.

"Ah," said the poor lover. "If I could only — somehow — take hold of your heart and make that mine, Kate! Sometimes it maddens me. Here I am with all my strength. There you are with all your weakness. But I can't make an impression."

"I have given you my promise, Henry. You don't doubt that that is sacred to me?"

"I can tell you this. I think I'd hold you to it without a scruple. That is how I love you. Without a conscience, Kate. The desperate fear of losing you — God in heaven, how it haunts me!"

She waited a moment with her heart beating in her throat. "Hush!" she said at last.

"I know. I'll say no more. I'm terribly sorry, dear."

"Not that. Only —"

"Tell me that I'm only half wrong."

"Yes, yet! Of course you are."

"But half right, too?"

"I — I don't quite know."

"That means you do know."

"Please don't say that. You are a little cruel, Henry, tonight."

"I'm a boor!" he groaned. "Confound it, I'm a fool and a rogue to plague you like this. I'll leave you, Kate. I'll try to rub some of my roughness before we meet again."

"Sit still," she said, "it isn't right for us to run away from such a thing as this. But just let's not talk about it for a little while. I wish — almost — that you hadn't started talking about it."

"So do I, in Heaven's name. Doubts will grow like any other weeds, once they are planted."

"You'll trust me to be honest?"

"As a man — more than any man I know."

"Then let's sit here a little — quietly. I feel as if a cannon had been booming. What a blessed thing the good old night is, Henry!"

He did not reply at once, but after a time he said in a faint, tired voice: "You were thinking of something a little while ago. Do you remember?"

"Yes."

"What was it?"

"Nothing of any importance. Would it please you to know?"

"Yes. So that it keeps us from talking about ourselves."

"Oh, it has nothing to do with us."

"I thought not," he commented bitterly. But she was so busy with that revived thought that she did not notice his tone.

"It was about gambling, Henry."

"That's one of your enthusiasms — against gambling."

"I don't know. Have you ever gambled?"

"Yes, of course. I have my vices, but that's not one of them."

"I wonder," said she.

"Do you doubt me?"

"No, I wasn't thinking of you."

"Oh!"

"Just about gambling itself. We're all gambling in a way."

"Why — you might say that. If a farmer sows his crop, he doesn't know just what return he'll get — a ten-sack crop or a one-sack crop. He may work just as hard. But bad weather will ruin everything. Or a man may sow his whole heart and all his soul in a woman and he may get in return — why, a ten-sack crop, or not even his seed back again. The — the crows may come and eat it all, you know!"

"Henry!"

"Forgive me, Kate. But I'm sick at heart. Let's go on with the gambling. I won't break in again."

"Perhaps we'd better stop talking."

"No, dear. I love to sit here and watch you. Your face is hardly more than a shadow to me, but there is the whiteness of your forehead molded in starlight, and that terrible, swift, tireless brain of yours working under it, dissecting things — dissecting me — finding God knows what — there I go again. But I promise not to be lost once more. I'll hew to the mark. Gambling — gambling — that's the thing. Talk some more about it."

"Well — if you wish."

"By all means. I'll try not to play the dolt. I'll promise not to."

"You're such a fine fellow, Henry!"

"Nonsense! But go on. Who put that idea into your head — about everything being a gamble?"

Instead of answering, she asked in return: "Did you ever know a gambler?"

"I used to know a man who later became one."

"What manner of person was he?"

"An odd sort. I knew him on the football field, a good many years ago. He was a dashing devil then, a free spirit if there ever was one."

"Ah!"

"That seems to please you, Kate."

"I know a gambler, too. He's like that. Like a knight — an adventurer, you know."

"H'm!" muttered Roland suddenly. "But slightly crooked, I suppose, like the man I'm referring to."

"Well, was your man dishonest?"

"Not in football. As game and as true a fellow as ever stepped. Fearless — he loved trouble and danger. Cool as good steel. A sword of fire to his opponents. He hewed me down among the rest one day. A captain and leader pouring heart into his own team. That was my man! Well, I saw him — afterward. He had the same cold, handsome face."

"Ah, they must be a type!" cried the girl. "This man — he is like that. He can keep all of his thoughts behind his eyes."

CHAPTER 21

All that was amiable in Henry Roland, all that was kindly, all that was generous was snuffed out of existence. He saw himself again on a far-off football field, smashing his way toward fame, struggling toward the goal posts, eager, resistless, with the crown of an athlete's glory just within the grip of his fingers, and then a slender figure in a blue jersey guarded with leather at the shoulder and at the elbow darting through the line of his interference, the crashing blow, the swallowing darkness. History repeats itself, said Roland to himself, and as Corcoran had wrecked his hopes once before — might he not do it again?

"Corcoran!" he exclaimed.

"You've heard of him, then?"

"Who hasn't heard of him!"

"What is it you have heard, then?"

"I can't tell you that."

"But you must, Henry. You have such an air of mystery that you make me guess at a thousand things. You must tell."

"I'm sorry."

"Don't be too irritating, Henry! I really want you to tell me what you know of him."

"My dear Kate, you can't expect me to slander your friends to your face."

She caught her breath. "Is it as bad as that?"

"Not a very pretty story as a matter of fact."

"If you've gone as far as this, of course you must finish it. As for him being a friend of mine — why, I've only seen the fellow once."

He breathed more easily. But before he could speak she added to herself, but aloud: "No, when he left me we *were* friends. You're very right, Henry. I must not hear slander against him when he cannot defend himself."

It was too much for all the good training and all the good resolutions of Henry Roland. He burst forth: "Good heavens, Kate, what are you saying? Friends with him? Why, he's a common gambler, a cheap — a trickster!"

"Well," murmured she, "you've said it at last. Give me your proofs, Henry!"

"Do you think enough of him to be angry because I've told you the truth?"

"Do you expect me to condemn any one before he has been heard in his own defense? That's not — square!"

It came out in a tone that made Roland straighten a bit in alarm. It was more serious than he had dreamed, after all. How could Corcoran have entrenched himself in the interests of this girl so quickly — the course of a single afternoon and evening while he was accomplishing so many other things?

"I'm telling you," he said, "what I've gathered from a hundred others. I'm telling you what every person in the town knows. Corcoran? He's famous in every town on the range. His foppery, his villainous trickery, his card sharping, his insolent audacity, his face of brass which refuses to be shamed. In the name of heaven, Kate, what have you been doing with your ears all this time, if you haven't heard of Corcoran and his doings?"

"Is he a lost soul?" asked the girl.

"Of course. Lost? He's a devil who tempts others. That's the truth about Corcoran."

He knew that he was outstepping the bonds of honesty; he knew that he was indulging in the first truly criminal impulse that had ever mastered him, and he thrilled with a wicked pleasure as he gave way to it.

"Corcoran? I tell you, there isn't a more

207

infamous name in the whole mountain desert, so far as I've been able to make out!"

She considered this for a long time. He had expected exclamations from her, and dismay, but instead, this considerate quiet alarmed him greatly. She was using the pause to weigh what he had said.

"At least," she said suddenly, "I think you are right about one thing. I think that he *could* be a very great villain."

"I'm telling you about an accomplished fact — not a possibility."

"I understand. But don't you think, Henry, that if his energies were used in the right way that he might become just as fine a man in the future as he has been a wicked one in the past?"

He waved his hands before him through the darkness. "Why, Kate, you are talking fairy-book stuff now. You don't really mean to say that you have put any faith in that renegade?"

"I do," said she. She was growing angry, now. "I think, in short, that he will prove himself a different man from now on."

"Why?" asked Roland.

"You'll see."

"At least tell me what I should be looking for."

"For one thing, you'll never see him gamble again!"

"Good heavens, Kate; who's been filling your head with such nonsense?"

"Henry, you talk as if I were actually witless."

"Don't get excited, please."

"I'm trying not to. But you're insulting, Henry. You really are. Please allow me to —" She stopped, ashamed for having gone so far in the wrangle.

"I'm very sorry," said Roland, much perturbed. "I've said more than I should have said. But — the idea of Corcoran not gambling again is really amusing. Can you imagine a fish breathing and living out of the water? That's the way it would be with him. That devil of a man, they say, is wretched unless he's ruining the lives and happiness of other men."

"That is very strongly put. You wouldn't like to be quoted, I'm sure."

"That's a rather ugly way to put it, isn't it? I say that I *am* ready to be quoted. I'll face Corcoran and tell him what I think — I'll —"

"Hush!"

"Kate, you drive me mad. You — Corcoran — my brain is whirling."

"Hush, hush! I've forgotten everything. Don't be foolishly excited."

"Only tell me this."

"Not another thing about it. Not until you've had a chance to sleep and think it over."

"At least — what made you think that he would give up gambling?"

After all, her reason for that statement had been ridiculous enough, as she could see now — the chance word of a strange man which she had accepted as the truth. But like some very proud people, she disdained hiding behind anything other than the truth. She laid her gullibility open to be laughed at — if he dared.

"He told me so himself. He said that he intended to give up gambling. He had already most freely confessed that he was a professional gambler."

A stifled groan from Roland. "What induced him to make the promise?"

She was silent, growing very red and hot of face, blessing the darkness which shielded her face. She had not thought the whole matter over before. She had not considered it carefully. Now it suddenly occurred to her as a most remarkable thing indeed that this gambler should have talked with her as he had done. She made up her mind to two things on the spur of the moment. The one was that she had been a fool to listen to him and to believe him — the other was a determination never again to trust a man unless Corcoran proved true to the promise which he had given her. With this perfectly contradictory and wholly feminine resolution, she looked grimly before her through the night.

She said: "I suppose he said that he would give up gambling because — because he saw that it was really wicked."

Roland was relentless. "What made him see the wickedness of it so suddenly?"

She was silent, hating Corcoran, hating all men, hating Henry Roland most of all.

"Here is an intelligent fellow," said Roland most stupidly driving on. "Here is a man with a sharper wit than almost any fellow I have ever met. And yet he suddenly comes to a resolution to reform; he sees that his ways have been evil for the first time — revealed as by a lightning flash. Really, Kate, it's too much."

"I can't ask you to believe me," she said through her teeth.

"I'm glad you can't. But of course we may as well be frank. Our gambler friend has grown very sentimental about Miss Kitty Murran — confound his impudent heart for it!" He rose from his chair. "I have to leave you, Kate," he said.

"Why? And not before you promise me that you and Mr. Corcoran —"

"Good-bye!" cried Roland, tortured by the use of that name again. He started for the gate. She stopped him hastily.

"Henry," said she, "if there is trouble out of this, do you know what it will come to?"

"What do you mean?"

"Two dead men! Something tells me that! He is too swift and deadly not to kill. You are too big and strong not to kill. You will murder one another if you ever fight. Do you understand? You'll murder one another, Henry! I want you to swear that you won't go near Mr. Corcoran —"

"I can't promise."

"Henry!"

"Will you believe, Kate, that I am going to do my very best to manage what is right and just — for you — for me — and for — for Corcoran!" His voice broke with hatred and with grief and with rage. And he hurried off through the night.

She followed him to the gate. There she watched his burly form fading into the darkness, and after that she went slowly back toward the house. On one side of her the big-striding bulk of Henry Roland seemed to stalk; on the other, the light step and the pale face of Corcoran. The battle had already begun. And if it did, whom should she favor?

She was struck with horror to find that she could not wish Henry Roland success!

CHAPTER 22

If he did not know, he could at least surmise all that was passing through the mind of the lady of his love. And as he strode away through the darkness, he was more maddened by the knowledge that he had stupidly pressed on the subject of the discussion until he had brought about the denouement.

His temper was fit for a murder, at that moment. But if he raged at himself he felt toward Corcoran as toward a poisonous dog. If he could find the fellow, he would destroy him.

Three burly miners loomed before him, walking with their arms linked, their heads high, not drunk enough to be stupid, nor helpless, but just drunk enough to be recklessly gay. As Henry Roland hurried around them the nearest man tripped him adroitly and sent him blundering half a dozen paces ahead. The three miners came on, still arm in arm, reeling with joyous laughter.

Roland struck out the laughter with his

first blow. He wheeled on his heel and stamped a broad, heavy fist into the face of the central member of the trio. The fellow went down with a crash, torn loose from the hands of his companions.

The others came in gallantly, but they were no match for a cool-headed fighter who had trained his bulk to the most effective fighting force. He hit them off their feet with stunning force and went on down the street leaving a huddled, writhing heap of groans and curses behind him.

That was some satisfaction, but he wanted more of the same sort before the night was over. He wanted to step through gore, so to speak, and above all, he wanted to set his hands upon Corcoran. So he reached the hotel and was shown at once to the room of Corcoran.

"Come in!" called the voice within.

He opened the door and saw Corcoran sitting with his head bowed in thought, his hands clasped one upon the other on top of his cane.

"Who is there?" asked Corcoran, like a sick man too weak to open his eyes.

That calm insolence turned Roland hot with new anger. He slammed the door heavily behind him and that noise made Corcoran look up, but only slowly, indifferently.

"You're upset, I see," said Corcoran. "Sit down, Mr. Roland."

"Burlington," began Roland, "what I want to tell you is that I —"

"I beg your pardon," said Corcoran. "What name did you use?"

"Damnation!" exploded the other. "Are you still to play this foolish game with me? I tell you, I have recognized you beyond the possibility of any doubt. However, if you prefer to be known under a false name, I'll call you Corcoran, or what you please!"

He half expected, at that instant, that Corcoran would reach for a gun. Far less than this, according to report, was ordinarily required to induce that ready gun to leap out of the holster. But Corcoran made not a movement.

He merely shook his head slowly and thoughtfully, at last, as though pondering the strange processes of the mind which could bring a man to such pointless conduct. He even condescended to express a regret, saying gently: "You are a bit off color to-night, my friend Roland. Sit down and tell me what had cut you up so terribly. I am sure that none of your old acquaintances would recognize you."

The reproof was sufficiently kindly and sufficiently subtle to bring the ready crimson to the cheek of Roland. However, having started the conversation with the headlong velocity of a cavalry charge, he could not keep from going on with it, in much the same fashion.

"Corcoran," he said, "we are about to have an understanding with one another."

"I shall be glad of that," said Corcoran, rising when he saw that his guest did not intend to be seated. He never seemed more dapper, more delicate of build, than when he confronted the big man. And in contrast with the handsome, bronzed features of Roland, his own face had never seemed so pale or so thin. "Especially," said Corcoran, leaning against the table and still toying with the ebony stick, "when I can find out what has excited you so much today."

"I shall be glad to tell you," answered the other. "What has excited me, Corcoran, is a report I have received concerning certain representations which you have made."

"Ah? Concerning you? I assure you that I have not had your name on my tongue since I saw you in town a few hours back."

"Not concerning me, but concerning yourself."

Bewilderment came in a shadow across the face of Corcoran.

"If what I said had to do with myself only

— how the deuce can it have upset you, Roland?"

"Because I am cast upon by these — misrepresentations."

"I hope that I did not understand that last word."

"Misrepresentation was the word I used," said the big man.

"It is very strong language," was the calm reply of Corcoran. "You seem to have come intent upon trouble."

"I hope that it may be unnecessary," said Roland. "However, we must attempt to get at the bottom of this matter."

"By all means."

"I am going to ask you, Corcoran, what thing you consider the most despicable in the entire world."

The answer came so pat that it staggered Roland: "The most damnable thing in the world, beyond all question, is two-face, horrible hypocrisy!"

"By the heavens, Corcoran, it is the very crime which I have come to bring home to you."

"Impossible!"

"I tell you, it is true."

"Understand me," said Corcoran, breathing with quivering, expanding nostrils. "I rarely go to the trouble of explaining myself. It is not a necessity in my life. But tonight — you may command me. Mr. Roland."

"I am a thousand times obliged."

Their voices were soft enough for any parlor conversation; but their faces were white and their bodies shaken by their rage.

"In the first place, Mr. Corcoran," went on Roland, "I may say that various bits of your reputation have floated to my ears since I came into the West. Of course, I did not recognize the name; I never dreamed that my old friend and rival of the football field — however, let that go! I say that since I arrived in the West I have heard a very great deal of the famous Corcoran. I have heard of his revolver which comes out like a lightning flash."

"A pleasant thought," said Corcoran.

"Of his accurate aim which has never missed his target in all his battles."

"Like the prince in the fairy story, Roland."

"Of the consummate horsemanship of this Corcoran."

"Rumor has been too kind."

"Of his remarkable — dexterity — with the cards."

"Of that," said Corcoran coldly, "I confess my pride."

"Ah? And of the singular fashion in which fortune has always favored you around tables covered with green felt —"

"I admit that distinction with the greatest pleasure."

"But I have also heard of your adventures of the heart. What, Corcoran, you rascal — a true Lothario — a breaker of hearts among these mountain girls — is that not so?"

"There is a broad lie which Rumor has told about me," said Corcoran. "I never have wasted much time among the beautiful sex, I can assure you."

"They make small difference to you?"

"Very small."

"You are one to pick and choose, however. Here and there your eyes fall upon a special favorite, a rare privilege to some girl to be permitted to hear your voice whisper — ah, Corcoran?"

"You are beginning to annoy me a little," said Corcoran quietly. "I wish you would not talk like this. Besides, what the devil are you driving at?"

"Why, at a very little thing, you cur! I am only driving at the miserable lies which you have been pouring into the ears of the woman to whom you knew I was engaged for marriage!"

As he exploded the latter part of this sentence, he whipped out his revolver at the same instant and covered his host with the weapon. The hand of Corcoran, however, moved with the most remarkable slowness. It went back most casually to his coat and slipped inside the breast, while he said in face of the quivering muzzle of the other gun: "What would you hit if you fired, Roland? Really, you must give less time to boxing and more time to gun play. You would be very apt to send a bullet through the wall, you know, your gun is shaking in your hand at such a rate."

With this, he took out his own revolver, so that there could be no doubt that his intentions were pacific, and he laid the gun quietly upon the table and then shoved it well out of his reach. After this, he turned again and faced his guest.

"However," he added, "I have no desire to kill you tonight. I have never yet drawn a weapon upon a helpless man, and I do not intend to begin now."

"Corcoran, you shall not be permitted to escape like this!"

A sort of spasm crossed the features of Corcoran. "Dear man," he said, "whatever lies have been told about me, they have certainly not forgot to put in one truth, which is that I have fought fifty times and never

221

failed to win; that I have faced danger a hundred times and never turned my back — danger, Mr. Roland, compared with which your threats are no more than whispering in the wind on a June night. No more than that, upon my sacred honor!"

Not even the headstrong fury of Roland could stand before the bitter and quiet scorn of this speech. He winced back a little in spite of himself until his recollection of what the girl had told him returned to spur him on again.

"Corcoran," he exclaimed, "you went so far on the first day you knew her as to let her imply that you would give up your gambling habits for her sake. It was most cowardly and unfair! You had heard about the foolish girl's desire to help others. You wanted to let her open her heart on you. On *you,* Corcoran. It's too ridiculous. You must have been convulsed with laughter as you heard her talk!"

"On the contrary," said Corcoran, "I give you my oath that I never before listened to any person with so much reverence, with so much respect, with so much absolute desire to have her see the truth about me and the whole truth."

"You are going to try to draw me into the heart of the fairy-tale?"

"I mean, Roland, that I have actually determined to give up gaming."

"For what reason?"

"You are losing control of yourself, Roland. I warn you that I can see it in your eye. Take care and do not go too far."

"Do you threaten me?" gasped out Roland.

"I speak to you absolutely impersonally."

"I have asked you a question. Do you intend to answer me?"

"If I can."

"Tell me, then. What is your reason for giving up gaming?"

"She may have told you before this."

"I do not care to remember what she told me. But — I may state that I inferred from what she said that your reason for giving up gaming had something to do with you — your friendship for her!"

"Roland, you are going mad with spite and anger. I shall talk with you no longer."

"By the heavens," thundered Roland, "it is true. You have dared to raise your eyes to her and juggle your words with her even after you knew that she belonged to me."

"You surprise me. *Belongs* to you?"

"Corcoran, you have done your best to poison her mind against me."

"I?"

"You have tried your damnable trickery and succeeded —"

"Succeeded?" cried Corcoran, with such a strange uplifting of his body and of his voice that at any other time Roland would have paused to wonder at it. "It is possible that she may have opened her eyes to some of the truth about you?"

"What truth?" thundered Roland, striding nearer.

"This — that you are a hopeless boor, my dear fellow!"

"To the devil with you!" gasped out Roland, and struck him down.

He fell heavily against the wall, lurched forward to his face upon the floor, and lay motionless with his arms thrown out.

As for Roland, he looked down upon his handiwork with a sort of horror mingled with wonder, as though he could not realize what had been done or that he, of all men, had done it. Then he ran his glance over the frail body. Certainly two such men could have been carved out of his own ample frame. And he felt as he had felt in his school days when he had been tempted into striking a smaller boy. He drew back toward the door. At least he could thank God that no one had seen this thing. And certainly Corcoran would never report it. He reached

the door, opened it hastily, and fled down
the stairs three at a time, as though the bodi-
less ghost of Corcoran were flying at his
heels.

CHAPTER 23

It was a long minute before Corcoran recovered himself enough to brace his body upon a trembling arm. Then he pushed himself into a sitting posture and let his upper body fall back against the wall. After that the recollection of what had happened served as a stimulant to recall his wits. He staggered into an upright position and clutched at the revolver; he reeled with it toward the open door of his room. But the well of the stairs was an empty pit of blackness, and there was not a voice or a human sound in the hotel.

He closed the door and went back again into the room. Even the light of the lamp was too much for him. He blew it out and sat in the black of the night. Only the window was visible, a dim rectangle yawning upon the outer dark. And Corcoran turned the matter slowly in his mind, like a weak man fumbling at a heavy weight.

He must kill Roland. But if he killed

Roland, he would be robbing the girl! Robbing her of what? He told himself at first that it was nothing — that Roland was a heavy boor, a hopeless fellow. But he knew better, and in his heart of hearts he was bitterly aware of all the sound and worthwhile qualities which the big man possessed.

There was nothing wrong with the soul of Roland. No matter what he might be betrayed into doing by an outburst of temper, probably no one in the world could have been more ashamed of what had been done this day than was big Roland himself. He was that manner of man!

With that gloomy consolation he walked the room again, then flung himself on the bed. But the bed was hot. The pillow was like a fire beneath his head. The coarse spread burned his hands. He slipped from the bed to the floor and lay there crosswise, his arms thrown wide, his eyes staring into the velvet thickness of the night through the room.

The wind stirred at the window, died, stirred again. There was a softly prolonged rustling, and Corcoran, turning his head a little, saw in the window, outlined against the starlight of the outer night, the faint figure of a man crouched on the sill, peering into the room.

It was like a crouched beast ready for the spring and the kill, at first. Then it dissolved into the body of a man waiting and watching there. Corcoran could see the stealthy turning of the stranger's head.

After that, the man from the night advanced a leg over the window sill. So infinite was his caution that it was a full minute before his foot touched the floor. It was an equal space before he had advanced his body through the square of the window. Finally he stood erect inside the room and began to move toward the bulky outline of the bed. He made a shadow against a shadow, no more.

In the meantime, as a cat prone on the floor gathers itself when it sees an indiscreet mouse venture out from a corner hole, so Corcoran gathered himself, turned on his side, and rose to his knees. And as the cat stalks, so stalked Corcoran, with his limbs gathered under him, ready to leap.

He circled behind the stranger, and as the man reached the bed, Corcoran rose softly to his feet. From the hand of the other he saw the dull glimmer of steel depending — a knife or a gun, he could not tell which. He had drawn his revolver long before, and now, as he leaped, he swung the heavy weapon up and down. The sound of the blow was dull and thick, crashing through the hat and against the head of the interloper. He fell in a crumpled heap. There was no need of a second stroke. Corcoran went deliberately to the table and kindled the lamp; when he turned again, he saw the body of his night assailant lying in a deformed, loose mass, and the face which he beheld was that of none other than his former visitor — Gabriel Dorn!

He took the fellow by the nape of the neck and lifted him. The sagging body stretched out like an accordion being extended, and Corcoran flopped it on the bed. Then he dipped the end of a towel in his water pitcher and whipped it across the face of Dorn.

The worthy artist gasped, gagged, and struggled to sit up. But when he found himself confronting the keen eyes of Corcoran, he shrank away against the head of the bed and raised an arm as though to shield himself from a blinding light.

"You have come back sooner than I expected," said Corcoran cruelly. "Perhaps you forgot something, eh?"

The wild eyes of Dorn rolled toward the lamp and back again as he grasped at this hope.

"There was a sketch —" he began.

Corcoran pointed to the floor where the revolver had fallen from the hand of Dorn, and seeing that mute and damning witness against him, the latter could not finish his appeal. He merely raised a hand toward his bruised head and his eyes became like the eyes of a dog which sees the whip raised in the hand of the master. Twice his white lips strove to frame words before he could say at last: "Corcoran — I — what do you think you'll do with me?"

"I don't know. I'm making up my mind just now. You came back to murder me, Dorn."

"No, no!"

"What will you call it, then?"

"Give me a chance to explain —"

"That you resented being kicked downstairs."

"Not that. I didn't resent it. I swear I didn't resent it, Corcoran."

"What was it that brought you, then?"

"I'm a poor man, Mr. Corcoran!"

"Except for what you steal from those who pity you — such as foolish schoolteachers and the like, eh?"

"I have lived a wicked life," groaned the sneak.

"Now you repent."

"Ah yes, Mr. Corcoran. It is never too late

for repentance. I *do* repent. And I was tempted."

"You had hoped to get my cash, I suppose."

"Not that. I had no intention of robbing you."

"Of anything more than my life?"

"They tempted me, sir!"

"Stop that!" commanded Corcoran, as the face of Dorn wrinkled with the agony of self-pity, and tears formed in his eyes. "If there are any tears, Dorn, I'll turn you over to the sheriff forthwith. Do you know what will happen then?"

"A sentence — a prison sentence?" muttered Dorn, wringing his hands. "I could never survive a year behind bars. A man with my sensitive soul —"

"No prison, Dorn. You need not worry about that. For a midnight murderer the people of this part of the country do not believe in even a long trial. They will stretch your neck on the nearest tree, Dorn! I am telling you the simple truth."

"And nothing for the people who sent me here?"

"As a matter of fact," said Corcoran, keeping as much of his contempt from his face as possible, "I think that if you informed on the others, you might be pardoned entirely. Tell me, Dorn, who could have been fool enough to trust such a job to you?"

"It was Rankin," gasped out Gabriel Dorn.

"Fat Ted Rankin?" mused Corcoran, sitting down on the foot of the bed. "Fat Ted Rankin! He has come to this, then? Hiring thugs to keep from paying his debts? Where did he find you?"

"In the street after he came out from the hotel. He stopped and looked at me for a while. Then he asked me if I intended to put up with what had happened to me when you — you —"

"Kicked you downstairs," suggested Corcoran brutally.

"That was it. I told him that I had been — er — greatly at fault and that — ah — that is to say, there was some justification for you when you —"

"In a word, Dorn, you answered him that you intended to cut my throat for what I had done to you!"

Dorn blinked. But apparently Corcoran had hit so near the truth that the artist went on as though the last words had been his own.

"Rankin said that he could give another good reason for getting rid of you. He took me to his place and we sat down in his own office. He was very firm about it. He said that you — that we must combine to get rid of you. I told him that — er — it seemed a rather difficult job. But he answered that it would be extremely simple if a man had only a certain amount of nerve — because you were so self-confident that you scorned to take precautions. He said that if a man dared to enter your room after the lights were out — that he would find it a simple matter —"

"Go on, Dorn. To slaughter me while I lay asleep."

"In short, it was something like that! But I objected that there was always danger with a terrible — fighter like you, and that I was not a fighting man myself."

"You seem to know yourself, Dorn."

"He said that he would give me reasons for making myself a fighting man. And he began by offering me two hundred dollars."

"As cheap as that? By the Lord, I should have thought that my life was worth more than that!"

"Do you think that I would have done it for any such amount?"

"Good! You bucked him up a bit, then?"

"By all means; I told him that I was not a fool. I told him that I would not dream of attempting such a thing for such an amount, particularly since Ted Rankin is rolling in money. He offered me three hundred and I told him that three hundred was nothing to such a man as he, but he told me he had lost heavily lately. Finally we compromised and fixed it at five hundred."

"As much as that!" murmured Corcoran.

"He spends money like water," said Dorn with dark enthusiasm. "He even paid me — a hundred dollars down before I took a step. I was too clever to go off without some sort of a payment beforehand!"

"Very well, then. Rankin bought you for five hundred dollars. So far, so good. You were to enter this room, shoot me through the head while I lay asleep, and then sneak off through the window again."

"In general, that was the idea."

"You can put that all in writing," said Corcoran.

"In writing?" breathed Dorn.

"Certainly. You might change your mind after a while. Some of the facts might grow dim in your memory. Much better to clap it all down in black and white at once, you know!"

"Ah?" murmured Gabriel. "That would be enough to hang me! You can't ask me for that, Mr. Corcoran."

"However, I must have it, Dorn."

"Do you mean to make me write by force?" groaned Gabriel Dorn.

"Exactly that, my fine friend. By force if need be. By very brutal force if need be, Dorn!"

With this, he picked up the slender ebony cane and made it whistle significantly through the air. Dorn backed against the wall in a panic, and at the same time, hearing a footfall passing softly down the outer hall, he suddenly raised his voice in a piercing scream for help.

That yell so astonished Corcoran that for a moment he could not stir. But when he saw Dorn rush for the door, he leaped after the rascal and caught him by the neck. At the same time, the door was thrust open, and into the room came half a dozen men with the formidable sheriff himself in the lead.

"Sheriff Nolan!" screamed Gabriel Dorn.

"Shut you that fool squealin'," said the sheriff without undue emotion. "Shut it up and sit tight, you blockhead. I got no room in my head for thinkin' while you're yappin' away like that. Now set down and rest your voice and tell us what's wrong in this here place. Dog-gone me if I didn't think that somebody was gettin' a throat cut by the yowl that you let out a minute ago."

"Corcoran —" stammered Dorn, and for the moment could say no more. He only clung to the sheriff's arm.

"Damn!" said the sheriff, "can't you pretend that you're a man for the half of a minute?"

"Stand between him and me!" pleaded Dorn.

"You see he ain't aimin' to lay a hand on you, you fool! He's standin' quiet and doin' nothin'."

"If he draws a gun —"

"He ain't goin' to draw no gun," said the sheriff.

"My blood," cried Dorn, "will be on your head!"

"All right," said the sheriff, "we got that all settled, then."

He turned to the others. "Set yourselves down, boys, and get easy. And shove that door shut. I ain't got quiet enough to hear myself thinkin'."

The door was closed in the face of twenty eager-eyed men who had heard the yell and the disturbance which followed. There remained in the room only the sheriff, some ten helpers who had leaped out of their beds and come in their bare feet, with their guns, ready for any manner of battle which might be offered, together with Corcoran and Gabriel Dorn.

Gabriel, in the meantime, could not be pushed away from the sheriff. He clung to Mike Nolan as to a rock of salvation, and stared timidly around him at the rough faces of men who had been roused out of a sound sleep and who came with their hair on end, their eyes wild, their brows knotted. There is nothing so savage as the face of a man newly awakened.

"Now," said the sheriff to Dorn, "tell me what all this deviltry is about, if you got sense enough to talk English."

"Corcoran —" choked out Dorn.

"We know he's in it. Look alive, man. He ain't goin' to eat you. Here's eleven men, countin' me, that got their guns ready to blow him to bits if he makes a move for his revolver. Y'understand? You're safe as if you was in — jail!"

This dreadful word made the whole body of Gabriel Dorn quake, and his face turned to a dull, dirty yellow.

"Sheriff," he breathed, "it was — it was — it was about Miss Murran —"

"Easy!" exclaimed the sheriff, starting suddenly away from his man and striking the clinging hands of Dorn off. "If you try to mix the name of — that lady — in this here game, darned if I won't get your neck stretched for you. And I'll be the first man to pull a rope!"

There was a brief, stern murmur from the others, and the worthy Gabriel groaned with terror.

"I'll say nothing," he moaned. "You don't want to hear me!"

"Talk out," said the sheriff. "I was just givin' you a warnin'. Now talk it right out. Name anybody you please — so long as you're tellin' the truth."

"The truth?" said Corcoran suddenly. "Look at him, sheriff. Do you think that cur is hunting for the truth?" and he pointed disdainfully at the quaking body of Dorn.

But the latter had been goaded too far. Like the rat which is concerned, he now leaped to an erect position and turned upon Corcoran with a face writhing and blackened with hatred and poisonous malice. He thrust out his arm and shook his lean forefinger toward Corcoran.

"It's Corcoran! It's all Corcoran!" he yelled. "He's lost his head about Kitty Murran. He's gone crazy about her. And — to get rid of Roland — to get rid of Roland

— he offered me five hundred dollars to murder Henry Roland tonight and wanted to kill me when I told him that I wouldn't do his dirty job!"

CHAPTER 24

Then, as he uttered the lie, he fell groveling on the floor begging the sheriff to keep him from the gun of Corcoran. The sheriff looked in scorn at the skulker at his feet. Then he turned to Corcoran. The latter sat on the edge of the table swinging his leg and smiling upon the company. Not a muscle of his face had changed during this crucial moment.

"What should be done with a liar of this nature, sheriff?" he asked Mike Nolan. "Or does it seem possible to you," he added, "that a sane man could send a cur hunting a lion?"

He looked quietly around him. But the faces that stared back at him were iron. The many faults of Henry Roland were well known. They were the faults to too sensitive a pride, and a man which was sometimes a little superior, sometimes a little condescending. These things had always been held strongly against him by the Western community. But his virtues had fairly forced themselves to attention. His courage, his generosity, his open hand, his kind heart had been published not with clamor but by a thousand little acts of good nature which gradually had been spread abroad. They did not realize how greatly they esteemed him until, at this moment, they heard a plot against him announced. So it was that they glared back at Corcoran with solemn brows. He was amazed and startled by their gravity. The whole affair seemed to him too ridiculous to be worth considering for a moment. He forgot, for the moment, that he was in a time and a country where men were accustomed to even stranger things — where one might go to sleep a poor man and wake up rich — where wealth was being reaped from the dirt itself! The ridiculous nature of the charge which was brought against Corcoran did not seem to have impressed a single one of those stern-faced men who sat in the room with him. They did not murmur against him, but they looked grimly upon him, illustrating how foolish is the law when it declares that no man is considered guilty until his guilt is proved. The taint had been placed upon Corcoran. He saw that it would remain on him until he removed it.

He said to the sheriff: "I want to cross-question this fellow. May I?"

"Blaze away," said the sheriff. "Heaven knows I hope that you can unprove what he says."

"Wait, sheriff. It's not up to me to prove my case. It's up to Dorn to prove his. Isn't that the law of the matter?"

The sheriff scratched his head. "The law is a dog-gone funny business," he said. "You might say that I've been hitched up to it about the half of my life, but I never got friendly with it. It never done me no good that I know of. I've kept clear of it as much as I could. I dunno what the law says. I know what we've heard this Dorn, here, say!"

The other men nodded.

"Stand up, Dorn," said Corcoran at last.

Dorn looked at the sheriff and the sheriff shuddered, so greatly did the cowardice of this man sicken him.

"Get up and stand on your two feet. Get up on your hind legs, Dorn! He ain't goin' to eat you. Not while we're standin' by!"

Dorn rose and stood on sagging, shaking legs.

"Now, Dorn," said Corcoran, "try to tell a straight story, because I'm going to trip you up and make you tell the truth if I can. I have been talking to you about Roland, have I?"

"You have," gasped out Dorn.

"Very well. Put it all in my words. Tell me exactly what I said to you."

The eye of Dorn rolled wildly, but it did not roll in vain. When he looked at Corcoran again, there was inspiration in his face.

"You said: 'Dorn, I want to talk to you about a private affair of mine in which —' "

"Wait," broke in Corcoran, "I see that you're a more fluent liar than I thought. We'll begin in a different way." He paused, scowling straight at Dorn. "How did you come into this room just now?"

"Why, through the door, of course. How else would a gentleman enter the room of a — friend?"

"Gentleman?" said Corcoran softly. "Friend? Well, well!"

Even the stolid miners who sat about the room were impressed. The confidence of Corcoran would have moved a mountain to sympathy. Besides, they detested cowardice as the worst of vices. And their detestation poisoned their minds against Dorn.

"You did not climb in through the window, Dorn?" continued Corcoran relentlessly.

"No," breathed Dorn.

But he shrank before the sudden centering of attention upon him. The lie stood almost in his shifting eyes.

"When you had slipped carefully through the window, you did not sneak along that wall toward my bed?"

"No," whispered Dorn, opening his shirt at the throat for the sake of freer breathing.

Corcoran stood up from the table and pointed.

"You were not carrying that gun in your hand?"

All eyes swung to the side of the room. There lay the long, ominous form of a six-shooter close to the wall. They looked back to Dorn with a murmur of angry impatience.

"Talk, Dorn," said the sheriff. "I'm kind of hankerin' to see what you got to say to that! Dog-gone me if I ain't gettin' suspicious of somethin' pretty dirty here!"

"For Heaven's sake, gentlemen," said Dorn, "believe me! I did not do what he says!"

"You did not go to the bed and lean over it?" said Corcoran. "You did not stand there looking for me, with the gun in your hand?"

Speech was for the moment impossible to Dorn. He could only shake his head with a nervous violence.

"I did not," went on Corcoran, "jump on you from behind, out of the darkness, and knock you down with the butt of my gun?"

"No!" gasped out Dorn.

"Very well! Then what brought that bump on your head? What did that, Dorn?"

Poor Gabriel Dorn looked wildly about him.

"Talk up," snarled out the sheriff, growing more and more irritated as the picture of the midnight attack was painted more clearly in his mind.

"Gentlemen," said the trembling culprit, "will you try to believe me while I tell you the naked truth?"

"Talk out!" growled the sheriff. "We'll see about the believin' after we've heard what you got to say."

"It was like this," said Dorn, breathing deeply as though fear had more than half choked him. "I had a disagreement with Mr. Corcoran earlier in the evening. Afterward he met me in the street and said that he was sorry for what had happened."

"Where did you meet me on the street?" asked Corcoran.

"About fifty yards from the hotel," said Dorn, blinking, but talking smoothly enough. "Near the corner by the —"

"Go on," said Corcoran, "you lie better than I thought you could."

"Mr. Corcoran told me that he was in

great trouble and asked me to come to his room later in the evening — when everything was quiet. He did not want any one to see me enter his room, and he said that the signal for my coming would be when I saw the light put out in the window here."

He paused for breath. The sheriff's face was still stern, but the tale was so glib that he listened with patient interest. And after all, there was cause for interest. Here was a man's life hanging by a most meager thread. If the story of Corcoran were true, nothing that the sheriff could do would prevent the miners from hanging Dorn to the nearest tree. Obviously the fellow was fighting for his life. So all the group listened with intent interest and said not a word, merely glancing at one another significantly when important points were made.

"I waited until the window was dark, accordingly," said Dorn, gathering more strength of voice as the heat of the invention grew upon him, "and then I came quietly into the hotel. There was no one in the lobby except Juan Marmosa, sound asleep in a corner, and —"

"Well," broke in the sheriff, "that's true enough. I seen him there as I come through and they wasn't nobody else around."

This confirmation seemed to tell heavily

in the favor of the narrator. Perhaps, thought Corcoran, he had glanced into the lobby before clambering up toward the window of the hotel.

"I came up to Mr. Corcoran's room," said Dorn. "When I rapped at the door, it was opened on the dark. I went in — I was a little nervous, gentlemen —"

A broad grin ran around the circle of listeners, and they nodded.

"Being alone in the dark with such a man as Corcoran, with his reputation — I am a peaceful man, sirs —"

There was another responsive grin.

"I asked him to light a lamp, and he did it. Then he told me very bluntly what he wanted me to do. He said: 'You're a poor man, Dorn.' I said I was, but that I considered honest poverty no disgrace —"

"Get on with the facts," said the sheriff, "and stop pitying yourself."

"Yes sir. Very well then, he told me that I could make five hundred dollars very easily. I told him that there was almost nothing that I would not do for five hundred dollars. Then he told me that Henry Roland stood in his way. I asked him in what manner, and he said it was on account of Kate Murran. He had seen her and —"

"You rat!" exclaimed Corcoran, quivering with sudden rage and scorn.

"Sheriff Nolan!" cried Dorn, shrinking toward the man of the law.

"Steady, Corcoran," said the sheriff. "We got to hear this feller out to the end now that he's started."

"He'd seen Miss Murran," said Dorn in a trembling voice, but with his face beginning to wrinkle with venom, "and he'd walked home with her from my house, as I happen to know. He told me that she should not be wasted on a thick-headed fellow like Roland and that he wanted to get Henry Roland out of the way. So he offered me five hundred dollars if I'd go to Roland's room and —"

"Send you to Roland?" sneered Corcoran. "Send a coward to do a brave man's work?"

"He said," stammered Dorn, "that a known man would not have much of a chance, but that because it was known that I was not a fighter, I might be able to get behind him —"

There was a growl from the listeners. Plainly they were beginning to take stock in the narration of the coward.

"I told him frankly that I did not like the idea. I — I was afraid to express my opinion of — of such a dirty thing — more openly."

He paused and then went on, boldly

staring at Corcoran.

"He seemed to think that I only needed a little more temptation, and then he drew out money and offered me a hundred dollars. I took it before I knew what I was doing, and put it in my pocket. Then he told me that I would get the rest when the work was done. I told him that I would never attack another man — then he broke into a fury. He said that if that was the case, he'd never let me leave the room alive to talk about what he had said."

"You dog!" cried Corcoran, feeling the ground slip fast from beneath his feet.

"He jumped at me, then, and struck me down with his revolver just as I, in desperation, was drawing mine. I screamed for help, and —"

"We heard you yell," said half a dozen voices, as the speakers looked across the room to Corcoran.

"In the name of heaven, sheriff," said Corcoran, apparently more angered than alarmed, "are you going to believe such a cock and bull story? That I would hire a fool like this and a fellow who is more woman than man to attack such a man as Henry Roland? Roland would break him in two and throw the pieces away!"

The sheriff nodded, with a frown. It was

apparent that he was bewildered by the whole problem.

"And yet," broke in Dorn desperately, "he asks you to believe that I'd come to attack a man who is known to be ten times the most dangerous fighter in the mountains. If I am not brave enough to attack Henry Roland, what under heaven could make me brave enough to attack, as he says I did, such a terrible fighter as Thomas Corcoran is known to be."

The sheriff started, so keenly did that suggestion tell in his mind.

"By Jimmy crickets," muttered Nolan, "that's true. I didn't think of that before. Corcoran, how do you answer that?"

But Corcoran, for the moment, was too amazed to find his tongue. And that fact, he saw, was joined to all that had been said before to tell against him in the minds of those who were listening and sitting as an impromptu jury in that case — a jury which was exceedingly apt to bring in a judgment and then summarily to execute it.

"Gents," said one man, speaking with a sudden rough voice, "whichever way this here thing works, it looks like one of these two gents deserved the free use of a rope. Darned if I wouldn't donate mine without no charge!"

"Well," drawled Nolan, "I've knowed this here gent, Mr. Dorn, for a considerable spell, and I dunno that anybody ever accused him before of havin' as much as a hundred dollars on him. He's accused himself of havin' that much right now. He ain't said that our friend Corcoran, here, had the time to take back the money that he said was give to him. Dorn, I'd sort of like to see the face of that hundred dollars."

"Yes!" muttered the rest. For here, at last, was tangible evidence on the basis of which they could make up their minds.

Dorn cried huskily, trembling with joy: "Gentlemen, I thank Heaven that I can prove my case. Here is the money!"

And he tore a narrow handful of money out of his pocket and waved it in the air before him.

CHAPTER 25

It was such a moment, as often comes in the courtroom when the defense has stood up long and valiantly against the attacks of the prosecution and when the witnesses for the State are unable to make any headway worth notice in the face of the stalwart denials of the accused. Then there may be found in some obscure corner one who has hitherto feared to make his knowledge public. He comes forward at last. He is sworn in. He stands before the judge and the jury. He looks at accused and accuser. And in swift easy words, stamped with the strength of the utter truth, he damns the man on trial. Every word he utters takes the prisoner a long stride nearer to the gallows. But at last his speech is ended, his story is complete. Even cross-examination is useless, and the lawyers for the defense merely hang their heads in despair or sit back in their chairs to admit that it is folly to attack a stone wall. Examination will simply make the case stronger against their client — hang him instead of giving him, perhaps, a chance to escape with a long prison sentence.

So it was in this moment with Corcoran. So much had been said that was unsupported by any evidence except the fallen gun and the blow on the head of the smaller man — so much had been said which had no solid evidence behind it, that it seemed with the production of the little handful of money that solid and permanent truth was established.

It was a small thing, but produced at that moment, it was decisive. So, when two armies lie locked and wavering in a strong battle, the brilliant charge of a little handful of cavalry is the touch which causes the wavering to turn to terror and then to the flight of a company — a regiment follows — a whole army is suddenly rushing across the field in rout, mad with terror. And so it was with the appearance of the money.

The sheriff rose slowly from his chair and stood transfixed, staring at the coin. He held out his hand. Into it he received the fluttering bills, stirred by the breath of wind which had rushed in through the window. The whole world, for the moment, had no more important thing to do than to gaze at that bit of money.

"It's here," said the sheriff slowly and

heavily. "God knows that I couldn't believe it of a gent like Corcoran. I thought this same evenin' that no matter what might ever be charged up again' him, it was only the things that was done by a gent that was too smart for his own good. I thought he was square. But here's the money. Seventy-eight-ninety — one hundred dollars in paper, gents, just the way that Dorn claimed."

He turned slowly to Corcoran.

"Sheriff," said the latter growing a little pale, now, in spite of himself, "you will have to admit that this is extremely circumstantial evidence —"

"I dunno about your smart language and your big words," said the sheriff. "I ain't no lawyer. All I know is the facts when I see 'em. Here's about a hundred facts, it looks like to me. I got 'em right here in my hand. I can feel 'em. And I can see 'em. I got 'em from Dorn, and he says he got 'em from you."

"Sheriff, use common sense. Couldn't he have received that money from the people who hired him to get rid of me?"

"Well," said the sheriff, with some heat, "I ain't ever pretended to be any smart aleck. But folks has always said that I had pretty good common sense. You're calling me a plumb fool."

"Sheriff—" But he saw that it was useless to talk, now.

"Gents," said the sheriff in his usual slow voice, "you might take a look over yonder to the window and see that there ain't too much attention paid to it in case of a little rush —"

Instantly three men ranged themselves before the window.

"Now," said the sheriff, "if I ain't got much sense, I hope that you're goin' to show enough to make you come along with us without making no fuss, eh?"

Corcoran looked sadly about him, and it seemed to him that all the evil deeds of his life looked back at him out of the eyes of the others. Had he one solid year of honest toil and honest effort behind him, he felt that it would have redeemed him there. But there was no such period in his record. All was a tale of waste. All was a story of sharp brains winning a living from the world at the expense of society to which he had contributed nothing — not so much as fair exploitation! A little act of generosity here and there — performed with money dishonestly obtained, that was all he could claim. And because of it, this tiny bit of evidence was enough to damn him, and enough to hang him.

"Certainly, sheriff," said Corcoran, "I am

not fool enough to make a disturbance in the face of such odds. Besides, I assure you that I have not the slightest perturbation. When Henry Roland is examined, he will say —"

He paused. What *would* Roland say when he was confronted with such news as this? Would he not recall their quarrel of earlier in that same eventful evening? Would he not remember the unjust blow which he had struck? Would he not feel that it might have incited Corcoran to take even a most cruel and cowardly revenge?

"What will Roland say?" pressed the sheriff.

"God alone knows!" said Corcoran sadly. "I feel that I cannot make sure of what any man will think or feel."

"That's sense," said one of the ten. "But speakin' of God, maybe it ain't goin' to be so long before you get your chance to have a look at him and hear his own opinion of you!"

There was a savage growl from the others, and at the sound, Dorn shrank into a corner. There he stood wringing his hands with terror and with delight. With terror because, but for the grace of fortune, he might himself have stood where Corcoran was now standing, with vengeance staring him in the face. With delight, because he saw the blow about to descend upon a man whom he hated with all his vicious soul.

"Steady, lads," said the sheriff hastily. "There ain't no call for you bein' all too dog-goned ready to help me. I don't need no help. When I get the cuffs on my friend Corcoran, here, I guess that he'll be safe enough with me."

Two men sidled in front of the sheriff and blocked him away from his man.

"Look here, sheriff," said one of them, "ain't it true that there's a good many slips in these here law courts? You take a smart gent like this here Corcoran, he's sure to have a lot of coin piled up. He can hire smart lawyers. Dog-goned if he hardly needs to have lawyers, he can talk so smooth himself. What sort of a chance would we have of havin' justice done to him by any judge? I'm askin' you that, free and plain!"

"Partner," said the sheriff, "it ain't no go."

"Why not?"

"When a gent is arrested, he's got to go to jail and let the law take its course. They ain't no way around that there —"

"Look here, sheriff, what kind of justice could he get? He'll have twelve men talk, and judge him, won't he?"

"Yes."

"Well, here's eleven of us. Ain't we as

good as any jury that ever sat still and heard these here lawyers turn what was true into what was lies?"

"Maybe we might be," said the sheriff slowly. "I dunno about that. I ain't no hand for the fine points of things. But I got to tell you boys that that man, yonder, is my prisoner, and that —"

"Wait a minute, sheriff, because you ain't arrested him yet!"

"I do right now. Corcoran, in the name of the law, I arrest you!"

"Very good," said Corcoran. "This seems to become a puzzle. I hope that you'll be able to work it out!"

"Oh," murmured the sheriff, "I'll make it out, well enough. I'll make it out. I ain't goin' to have no trouble with these here boys. I don't need no encouragement from you, Corcoran. Boys, stand back and let me have my man!"

"Look here, sheriff —"

"Why, don't you hear me tellin' you to stand aside?"

"Sheriff, you got to listen to reason."

"Who in the devil are you to tell me what reason might be? Who in the devil are you, old son?"

"A friend of yours that's always voted for you, Mike."

"Why, Jack, I know that. They ain't no man that I think more of than I do of you, old-timer. But don't be makin' a fool of yourself now. I mean to have that man, there. Stand aside and let me get at him!"

The sharp, shaken voice of Dorn spoke from the corner of the room.

"Stand aside, gentlemen. Let the sheriff have Corcoran. Let him take Corcoran to jail, from which Corcoran will escape. Or let Corcoran be tried and be acquitted by a jury which doesn't know everything that you know about Corcoran. Let him get free. Then what will happen to all of you? How long will you live after Corcoran is out? Is he the sort of man to forget what you've been trying to do to him to-night?"

There was no answer to this insidious remark, but every head nodded. For there was a keen force to the words, and they had told heavily against the slender man who stood by the table with his cane caressed between his hands, in front of the lamp, which cast his huge shadow across the room, swallowing the debaters who stood around the sheriff.

"For the last time!" said the sheriff. "Will you stand back?"

"Grab him, boys!" said a voice.

It came from Dorn. But they did not wait

to think from whom it came. They only felt that that command crystallized the intention which had already been forming in their minds. Instantly four pairs of hands were laid upon the good sheriff, and he was held helpless.

He writhed and friggled and cursed tremendously, but he saw at once that he was helpless.

"Interferin' with the law," he bellowed. "That's what it is. It'll mean about ten years for every one of you, and I'll make it a point to see that you get it, I tell you! I'll make it a point. Corcoran, are you goin' to stand there like a fool and see yourself get lynched!"

"Get Corcoran!" shouted those who already held the sheriff.

"What can I do, sheriff, against ten men?" said Corcoran carelessly. "Besides, it is better to die with good grace than with a struggle."

He was already seized upon either side.

"There is no need for violence," he said quietly to his captors. "I assure you that I do not pretend to the working of miracles. You have me securely enough, and I shall not attempt to heat myself or you by useless struggles. Just bring the sheriff along so that he may see a man die as a gentleman should!"

"Cool!" said one. "Gents, if this here had only been honest, he'd of been a trump card to play in any hand that I ever seen. Hey, here's the sheriff's own irons. We can use 'em on Corcoran."

"Certainly," said Corcoran, "and a very good idea."

With that, he held out his hands, the cane still clasped in one of them.

His calmness amazed them all, but it also made them careless. One sharp oath, one struggle from him and their muscles would have been iron, but behold! He was still half reclining against the table, with his hands held out to the iron which would make his resistance definitely impossible.

But as the brightly polished and plated handcuffs were held out before him, he snapped out of his relaxed position as a wolf starts in his lair when he smells mountain lion at the mouth of the den, or as a horse starts when he smells the green fields, or as a football player, let us say, starts from his place when the signal is called.

So Corcoran whirled from his place and doubled over. His first twist had torn loose the grips of the men who held him. His second movement was to bend straight over in that angle which all football men know is the best for a sudden thrust through the line. Driven home with the proper skill and speed and strength, even through braced and practiced athletes in a line, prepared for just such an attack, many a great half back has knifed his way through the line for the necessary yardage and the coveted touchdown. So it was, too, with Corcoran. Except that he did not have practiced athletes before him. If they thought of any danger at all, they thought of it materializing in the form of a drawn revolver. But what they saw was merely a flash of a man as he whirled and plunged at them.

As for their own naked weapons, what could they use them on? They turned to fire, and they found that the fugitive had already driven into the mass of their comrades. They could not shoot without infinite danger of killing a dear friend. They clutched their guns in one hand; with the other they caught at Corcoran. It was like catching at a greased pig.

Many a man on the football field had thought of that as the slender body of Corcoran was driven down the field. How doubly true was it now among these great, slow-moving men, equipped rather for the labors of the mines than for agility?

Their yell of alarm caused the door to be flung open. There were gathered in the hall a solid mass of men who had been gathered there to wait and to watch and to listen to what might transpire in the trial chamber.

Across their faces the supple cane of Corcoran whipped and cut like a knife, and as they shrank back, his body drove into their midst. They made a confused jumble. Those behind did not know what was happening. Before they were aware, their own confusion had blocked the pursuit, and Corcoran was down the stairs like a flash.

Onto the veranda he bounded. There was no difficulty in picking out the best horse in the line. It was a tall and splendid gray which seemed to shine with an inner light. Instantly he was on its back, and the roar of its hoofs began down the street.

CHAPTER 26

The surest and the cheapest passport to the free country of Trouble, may be secured at any time by slapping some Western town in the face. It is like tapping on the nest of a wasp. The wasp wears his wings and carries his sting with him. And your true Westerner may be relied upon to have a gun handy and a horse not far away — a down-headed mustang which, at need, is apt to run the legs off a blooded animal in a fifty-mile cross-country hike.

So it was that the empty main street of the town of San Pablo suddenly swarmed with riders flogging their horses in the direction of the fugitive. The news traveled faster than the flying feet of the mustangs, fleet though the latter were.

"They had Corcoran dead to rights. He faded out right in the hands of the sheriff and about twenty of the boys. He got away!"

Of course the pride of San Pablo could not stand for such a thing. They spurred madly in the pursuit and Steve Maturin swore that he came within sight of a rider driving southeast along the bank of the Mirraquipa after he had flogged his mount for half an hour. But his mustang could not keep pace with the man he sighted in the light of the rising moon, so that the other disappeared. No other person among the hard-riding men of San Pablo came within so much as distant eyeshot of the fugitive.

For this there was a most excellent reason. No sooner had Corcoran issued from the southern end of the main street of the town than he verged sharp to the left and galloped due east and then northeast up the rolling sides of Comanche Mountain. And the rush of mounted men shot out from San Pablo and opened into a broad fan whose nearest side was still half a mile behind him. In five minutes he was well out of eyesight or hearing.

He went on until he came to a trickle of water which could not be dignified by even the name of a creek. This he followed to its source and found that it issued from a well-kept vegetable garden some small acres in extent. There the industry of the owner had terraced the rich soil of the mountainside and the fragrance of newly plowed, moist ground was everywhere in the nostrils of

Corcoran, together with the overriding odor of onions. A little square dobe shack stood in the center of this ground, its walls mouldered toward the base by the spring rains so that the little house had a knock-kneed appearance. Corcoran fetched a half circle around it and came to it down the mountainside. Then he dismounted and tapped at the front door.

He was answered by a sleepy voice in Spanish, and he replied in the same tongue that he was bound from the mines to San Pablo, but that it was too late for him to complete the trip. So, presently, the door was pushed open and the owner blinked out at him. It was a broad shouldered, squat-built peon with little glittering black eyes. His unlaced shoes had been pulled hastily upon the wrong feet, which was made quite possible by their ample size. And in his hand he bore an ancient rifle, the guardian of the house for at least a generation.

Between his yawns he made Corcoran welcome, as soon as he discovered that there was only a lone rider. First he conducted the gray horse to a little shed which was already more than half occupied by the proprietor's mule. By the time the gray was fed, he had told his story. He made a livelihood selling vegetables in San Pablo and had done the same thing all his life. His good wife had died the year before, and after that, his son had gone to work in the mines because he was tired of peddling through the streets of the town. So that the labor of cultivating and of selling both had fallen upon the shoulders of Pedro. However, as he said: "Work, you know, does not hurt a willing horse, señor!"

They went back into the house. There was only one room, with a ladder pointing into the dark mouth of an attic. But all was so neatly cared for that there was nothing repulsive about this living-dining-kitchen-bedroom. Pedro Hermosa made coffee for his guest, and while the latter drank it, the host busily arranged a bed in a corner of the room. It consisted of goat skins laid over a thin straw mattress, with a blanket on top of all, and Pedro worked away as cheerily as though the stranger had a right upon him.

Corcoran, in the meantime, sat crosslegged in a corner and sipped the coffee. Every swallow was giving him a stronger right upon the simple peon.

"Pedro Hermosa!" he said suddenly, at last.

Honest Pedro whirled upon him, half frightened.

"All that I have told you of coming from

the mines is untrue!"

He had expected an exclamation of surprise, but Hermosa merely pointed to the clothes of Corcoran and grinned.

"Señor," said he, "the dust higher up the mountain is all red."

Corcoran smiled in turn; but he looked a little more sharply at his host. He was beginning to guess that there were more brains behind that slant forehead than he had at first surmised.

"Very true," said Corcoran. "Now, as for my horse —"

The good Pedro raised his hand. "It is an excellent horse," said he. "I know that it must have cost you a great deal of money."

"In fact —" began Corcoran, but the other broke in on him saying: "I know its value because it looks like the blood brother of Señor Mortimer's gray horse in San Pablo." And he grinned again at Corcoran.

"I believe," said Corcoran, laughing openly now, "that they are related."

"I am not surprised," said Hermosa.

"But I wish to let you know, Hermosa, that I intend to stay here with you for several days, perhaps."

"You are a thousand times welcome, señor."

"However, you must know that there are

people in San Pablo who would be very glad to know where they could find —"

"To curious people," said Pedro Hermosa, "I talk about vegetables. Besides, I am very lonely here."

"Well, Pedro, I see that you are a fine fellow. I am putting my life in your hands. In the meantime, you must take care of my money for me."

He took out his wallet and tossed it to Pedro, who caught it from the air, and it opened between his hands. At the sight of the thick sheafs of notes, he shook his head and stared back at Corcoran.

"Ah," said he, "was it for this?"

"No," answered Corcoran frankly. "They accuse me of a thing of which I am not guilty. But where people have seen much smoke, Hermosa, they are very willing to find the fire, at last."

The peon nodded gravely. Then he offered the wallet again to his guest.

"I am not a banker," said he.

"You must be one for me," said Corcoran.

"No, no, amigo. You are my guest, and therefore you are sacred in this house. However, the sight of money is a poison. My father died of it. I went once to the races in San Pablo and gambled and won fifty dollars. So much as that, señor, which was a great deal to a poor man. My father saw it and dreamed about it until the next year when the races came again. Then he took all his money. Three hundred and fifteen dollars! He took it all to the races and bet it. And he came back with empty hands. It was too much for him. He fell into a fever and died in a month. So you see, señor, that money is a sickness which may be caught like a fever. I shall never have it near me! Never! Only what I raise out of the ground with my potatoes and my onions and the rest. Money that grows out of the dirt is clean money. There is no other that is clean, señor."

He added suddenly: "A thousand pardons, amigo! I should say that the only clean money to me is that which grows out of the dirt. But wise men make it grow from their minds."

Corcoran shook his head. "Everything you say is a hundred times true," he confessed. "And I'll keep the wallet!"

So he put it back into his pocket. And after that he lay down on his pallet, shrugged his thin shoulders on account of the hardness of his bed, and fell into a sound sleep, straightway.

Pedro Hermosa regarded the sleeper for

some time with an eye whose brightness was perhaps not altogether kindly. He waited until the relaxed features and the limp body of Corcoran showed that he was plunged in perfect slumber. Then the peon removed his shoes and approached the stranger cautiously. It was no trick to find the wallet. The coat of Corcoran had been thrown by him on top of the blankets, and the Mexican had only to lift it and slide his hand into the pocket. There lay the wealth in his palm. There lay the owner. With the very gun at the side of the sleeping man he could accomplish his destruction and call it, if he wished, suicide.

All of these thoughts went rapidly through the mind of the good Hermosa, and while his brain was occupied with them, they showed like glitter and shadow commingled in his features. At length, however, as his wild little eyes roved about the room, his glance fixed upon the emptied tin cup which Corcoran had just emptied of coffee.

Pedro Hermosa shrank with dread and shame. Hastily he restored the wallet to the pocket. He crossed the room to his own pallet and sat down crosslegged on it. A slant shaft of moonlight fell upon his rough, uplifted face and showed it haggard with dread and with repentance.

For he who had disregarded the laws of hospitality — how black is the hell into which he sinks after death!

Then he looked about him like a guilty child, searching for something through which he could make amends. He took an extra blanket, therefore, and, stealing across the room he laid it delicately over the sleeper. After this, he seemed more at ease, and going back to his own bed, he was soon once more huddled under his blanket.

He closed his eyes, but sleep was lost to him for the remainder of that night. He was thinking of one thing only — in what words should he confess the full horror of his temptation when he spoke before the priest at confession?

He could not see, through the blanketing dark, that the eyes of Corcoran had opened, that the gambler had smiled in the secret night, and that he had then fallen into a true slumber.

CHAPTER 27

The efforts of the sheriff were not confined to a mere blind pursuit of the gambler. In fact, so soon as he found that Corcoran was mounted upon the gray horse, he himself refused to take horse. But he plied the telegraph wires. He put himself in touch with the town of Eugene in the northwest. He communicated with the town of Mirraquipa to the southwest, which was the probable direction of Corcoran's flight. And he was assured in both directions that many a man would be riding to search the countryside for the fugitive. In the meantime, the town of San Pablo did what it could to encourage a brisk pursuit. For it gathered together a number of its most prominent citizens the next morning, early, and subscribed an ample fund as a reward for the capture of the man. That subscription list was generously opened by Theodore Rankin to the tune of a round thousand dollars. He made a little speech at the same time.

"This is to prove, gents, that all gamblers and all gamblin' ain't crooked. What we want is the law — lots of it. And we're willin' to pay for what we want. Gents, here's a thousand for them that get Corcoran!"

He was not, however, greatly applauded, for San Pablo had sense enough to see that every blow which was struck at Corcoran would help to assure to Rankin the possession of the seventy-five hundred dollars which had been won from him on the night before by this same Corcoran.

In the meantime, Mr. Henry Pertwee Roland went to the house of Kate Murran and found her, since it was a Saturday, at home. She was in the garden, wrapped in a gingham apron, and she was equipped with a watering pot in one hand and a trowel in the other. A man's sombrero afforded a shade for her face and shelter for her head. It was as awkward a costume as could have been contrived for any beauty, but Kate Murran was one of those women who rise above a stage setting. She carried her own atmosphere with her, so to speak, in her glowing cheeks and her bright, keen eyes. She could have been herself in Arctic furs or on tropic lawns. And Roland, at the gate, worshiped her frankly.

She greeted him as though nothing had

happened between them the evening before. Women are that way. They seem to realize — except when they pout to be wooed into brightness again — that a cloud upon the face is not becoming. Therefore they avoid it. They learn that a smile is a weapon whose edge is never dulled by use. Therefore they are constantly equipped with one.

Perhaps she had slept much less than he after their interview; but it was equally certain that she did not show it. She greeted him with a friendly nod.

"There is a queer bug after these roses," she said. "I don't know what to make of it. I've tried everything from soap and water to poisons. I wish you could help me solve the problem."

Henry Roland sighed. He was so greatly relieved at being received without malice that he could readily have fallen upon his knees and given thanks to the God who rules the universe and all that is in it — even the hearts of women, from time to time. So he stood close to her with his hat clutched in big, twitching fingers.

"You've forgiven me, Kate," he murmured, "for being such an impossible person last night?"

At this, she smiled up at him. "We're being watched from a front window," she cautioned him, and he could not tell, to save him, whether she were smiling with him or at him.

"This pansy bed," she was beginning, "is lost in the —"

"Confound the pansy bed!" exclaimed Roland. "I've spent a night on the border of damnation. I've walked the floor up and down and up and down, wondering what manner of dolt you must be thinking me, if you were indeed giving me so much as a thought. And now I come here, desperate, to find out your judgment, and you talk — of pansies. Kate —"

"I have heard of what has happened," said she.

These abrupt turnings of the conversation worried him infinitely.

"You have heard of what?" he asked.

"About Gabriel Dorn — and Corcoran." She added suddenly: "And about you. I understand that you went to him after you left me, last night?"

"I did," admitted Roland.

"Well, what in the world is it all about?"

"You mean, his attempt to have me put out of the way?"

"Nonsense, Henry."

"It is nonsense? There is the oath of your friend Gabriel Dorn on it."

"Gabriel Dorn?" cried the girl, and all the scorn in the world was gathered and expressed in those two words. "Gabriel Dorn! Oh, Henry, when I heard what he had done, and how he shrank and begged like a whipped puppy — I don't see how they can take the word of that man for anything against —"

She paused, and Roland filled in: "Against a gambler?"

"Well?" said she defiantly. "Against a gambler, then! At least, he's a brave man."

"Hired assassination is not usually considered courageous."

"I'll tell you what, Henry —"

"Well?"

"I don't think that there's a thing in it!"

"The devil, Kate! Do you really mean that?"

"On my honor, I can't help meaning it! That Mr. Corcoran would actually hire such a — a creature as Gabriel Dorn has turned out to be, and send him to butcher *you* at night?"

"San Pablo is fairly well convinced of that. Eleven sensible men sat in the room last night and heard enough to convince them that Corcoran was guilty of such an idea."

"Eleven men!" exclaimed the girl.

"Eleven sheep! Eleven men called up in the middle of the night, with guns in their hands, what is their judgment worth? Nothing! Nothing! Nothing!"

She stamped once with each of the last three words and Henry Roland stared at her in bewilderment.

"You have become his champion," he said stiffly.

At this, she was a little abashed, but he grew more gloomy than ever when he saw the red flooding her face.

"I don't think that I'm his champion," she said, "except that every one else seems to have gone mad. Because —"

"Very well, Kate. Let me have your reasons if you please!"

"Why, simply that Mr. Corcoran certainly impresses me as a man who would never *have* to get help in his battles. I can't imagine him being beaten."

The hard right fist of Roland collected itself. He was remembering how that fist had crashed home upon its mark the night before. He was heartily ashamed of what he had done, and yet try as he would, he could not really wish it undone.

"Perhaps not," said Roland. "However, I won't try to press the point. They have raised several thousand as a price upon the head of poor Corcoran. I certainly can't keep malice against him after that."

He was reading her face eagerly, intently, as he made this announcement. And she, dreading to let him see what she felt, stared down upon the ground. She rolled a small stone out of its bed at the edge of the garden path and shoved it into a new niche.

"A price on — his head?" she asked at last. "Does that mean dead or alive?"

"I really suppose that it does. They don't seem to care very much how he's brought in so that he arrives. They're a rough lot in this town, you know!"

"I know, but dead or alive! That is too terrible, Henry!"

"I knew you would feel that. I do too, for that matter. Poor Corcoran!"

He forgot all the bitterness of his newborn jealousy in a wave of better feeling.

"Let me tell you, Kate, that I knew him once as a man who wore another name — a fine, clean name that was known to thousands. By Jove, Kate, there was a time when that name was a household word among the youngsters of the whole country. Well, he preferred to let that name die."

"What was it, Henry?" cried she. The bright enthusiasm in her face as she drank in his words stopped up his speech.

"He has asked me not to tell it," he said. "I cannot violate his confidence. Because, you see, he was once a gentleman!"

"Are you so sure," she answered with a sudden hotness, "that he is no longer a gentleman?"

It stunned poor Henry Roland. For it seemed to him that every avowal of her faith in the gambler was a direct blow at him.

"You consider him a man of honor in spite —"

"In spite of gossip. I detest gossip! He will live up to every real promise which he has made."

"My dear Kate!"

"Don't talk to me, Henry. It angers me!"

"But confound it, Kate, the last thing he promised was that he would be in front of the hotel in the main street of the town at noon to-day. Do you think that he'll be idiot enough to do that?"

"Yes and yes and yes!" cried Kate Murran hotly. "He'll be there and punctual to the minute."

Roland lifted his hat.

"I'll come later," he said quietly, "if I may."

But Kate Murran turned her back on him and stamped into the house and through it and so out into the rear garden, where the berry vines climbed over their trellises and where the wide-limbed apple trees scattered dim shadows across the ground. And there she found Willie Kern leaning against one gnarled trunk, wriggling his toes in the dirt and slicing long shavings from a white pine stick which he carried tucked under one arm.

He twitched the ragged brim of his hat to her but did not move from his place. And at the sight of him, she half forgot her other worries. There was something on his mind — a great burden which occupied it. What it might be was what she must learn if she were able; that it was really important she surmised by the absentminded gravity of his face.

CHAPTER 28

She always put on her pleasantest manner when she was talking with Willie Kern. Most good women do with boys; for the younger men are the better they like them. Besides, there is something to be feared in boys, something trenchant in their wit, something cold and cruelly observant in their eyes. There is only one way of disarming them, and that is to win their worship.

"You're not happy, Willie," said Miss Murran.

"Nope," said Willie, and sighed.

A terrible thought came to Miss Murran. Could it be a girl? She scanned again his round, freckled face and felt reassured. He was not yet of the age — not quite.

"Then what are you thinking of?"

The answer staggered her. "The same thing that's botherin' you, Miss Murran."

"The same thing — Willie, what do you mean?"

"Corcoran," said he, and looked up from

his whittling in time to see rose color flood the face of the teacher.

At this, he shook his head. "I know," said Willie.

"You know what, Willie?" she asked, very close to bad temper because of the undue hotness of her face which she knew was telling a story. If only the boy would not be able to read it!

"About you and Corcoran," said Willie.

"Good heavens!" gasped out Miss Murran. Then, rallying rapidly as she felt that she had no cause for guilty emotion, she managed to say: "What do you know?"

"Everything," said Willie without enthusiasm. "But Miss Murran, I ain't goin' to blab to nobody."

"What on earth you can know that concerns me and — and — Mr. Corcoran," said she, "I really can't imagine."

He made no response except to bow his head over his stick and resume the paring of it into transparent shavings.

"Will you answer me, Willie?" she cried at last.

"Sure," said Willie in surprise, "if you'll tell me what it is you want to know."

"I want to know — what ridiculous chatter has gone about the town connecting me with — the gambler?"

At this he pocketed the stick and the knife and, thrusting his hands into his pockets, he wriggled his toes deep into the cool, moist earth beneath the tree and regarded her sadly, as one removed to an incalculable distance.

"There ain't no talk," said Willie. "There ain't a word except what you could hear mighty free. But they damn Corcoran a lot, of course."

"They do?"

"They say that he ain't got no right to even look at a girl like you. Which I dunno if they're right, Miss Murran. Corcoran, he says that they are."

"He does?" cried she. "How does he dare —" She could not finish.

"Dare what?" asked Willie.

"Nothing," said Miss Murran, feeling that she had grown hotter of face than ever.

"Because," said Willie, "they ain't nothin' that he don't *dare* to do."

"I am really not interested," said she.

"Ain't you?" said Willie, cocking his head to one side and grinning at her.

"Certainly not!"

But his grin persisted. "Maybe," said Willie, "you wouldn't care whether he was took or not when they chased him?"

"I don't know," said she, "why I should

wish anything except justice should be done on him!"

"Well," said Willie, "they ain't caught him yet. But I guess that don't matter to you?"

"Of course not, Willie," she cried, tormented by the strange new emotions which were making her heart swell, "why do you talk like this?"

"You wouldn't care, maybe?" persisted Willie carefully, drawing off this scene with much enjoyment, "you wouldn't care maybe, if you was to know what he'd said about you?"

She was stung to the quick; and her heart beat faster than ever. "One always cares what is said by such a — such a — such a public character, Willie!"

"He says, ma'am, that they ain't nobody like you."

"Is he — criticizing me — in public, then?"

"What he says to me is confidential, between friends," said Willie.

"Still, you tell it to me."

"He wouldn't care about that, I guess."

"Has he asked you to be his messenger?"

"Sure he ain't. He knows that I couldn't remember half of what he says. He only used me for one message."

"Ah? Did he send one to me? And by you, Willie?"

"He knowed that I wouldn't blab."

She looked far away to the gap between the mountains which guarded the passage of the Mirraquipa River. Somewhere far off, riding through the heat and the dust of the desert on a stolen horse — riding his own death warrant, therefore — was Thomas Corcoran. How the picture of him flared before her eyes, with the cane dangling in his hand, perhaps, in lieu of a riding crop.

"He'd come down here to tell you himself," said Willie.

"Willie!"

"Sure — he come himself."

"When?"

"Just now."

"You mean — he's in San Pablo now?"

"Sure."

She felt her head whirl.

"Is he mad, Willie? What could have brought him here when they would shoot him like a dog — on sight?"

"You brought him, Miss Murran."

"I have never given him reason to believe — I —"

Willie watched her emotion with infinite pleasure. "It's all right, Miss Murran," said he. "I ain't goin' to tell nobody."

"There is nothin' to tell."

"It ain't no good," said Willie, shaking his head. "I guess they ain't no woman that wouldn't like him if he wanted 'em to."

"Because he's a professional gambler?"

"Because he's square."

"Except when he plays crookedly with the cards?"

"He never cheated no honest man."

"How can you tell, Willie?"

"By the looks of him. He ain't no coward. He's got a clean eye, like a two-year old that ain't never been rode, yet."

It was a rude description, but it fitted perfectly with the image that was floating in her mind's eye.

"Oh, Willie," cried the girl, "you must never whisper a word of these foolish suspicions of yours. Of course, no matter what you think, the man is nothing to me. I've hardly seen him."

"Does it take a lot of lookin' to know the right sort of a man, Miss Murran?"

"Of course it does."

"Well, a gent could tell a hoss in one look and a dog in two."

"What can you tell about Corcoran, then?"

"That he's square, that he ain't got no

yaller streak in him nowhere, that he'd fight a dog-gone lion for a friend, and that his friends own him about as much as he owns himself."

"Who *are* his friends, Willie?"

"I dunno, except you and me."

"Do you insist on including me?"

"Sure," said Willie. "Oh, I guess I know!"

She pressed a hand across her eyes. That steady, relentless voice of assurance from the boy was driving home certain thoughts in her mind which she had hardly thought existed in her consciousness a little time before. Corcoran — Corcoran — Corcoran! He was at her elbow, his voice was at her ear, and every glimmer of sun among the leaves was the shining of the slender ebony cane. Corcoran! It was like hypnosis!

"Still in San Pablo! The madman!" whispered Kitty Murran.

"He come to see you."

"By broad daylight!"

"Then he seen you talkin' with Mr. Roland in the garden. He comes back to me and he says: 'Willie, I wanted to see Miss Murran. But there is some one else with her, just now. Will you remember to say to her what I tell you?'

"I told him that I would.

"He says: 'Tell her that Dorn has lied

shameful about me. Tell her that I am not beaten yet. Tell her, for the sake of kindness, to keep a bit of friendliness for me.' "

"Did he say that?"

"That was the way he begun."

"What else did he say?"

"He said: 'When you say it, Willie, remember that she is more to me than all the gold in Comanche Mountain or all the blue in the sky —' that was the way he begun. I dunno that I remember all the other things that was less than you! Miss Murran, I wished that you could of heard him! It sounded mighty fine. I allowed that I hoped you and him would get along pretty fine."

"I don't care to hear any more, Willie," exclaimed Miss Murran.

"But he says to me," went on Willie: " 'Perhaps I'll never see her again. God knows.' Like that he said it — sort of sick and weak. But I says to him: 'Dog-gone it, Mr. Corcoran, stories don't end that way.'

" 'Ah, Willie,' says he, leaning on his cane, 'this isn't a book. But I wish to Heaven that it were, and that you had the writing of it, because, in the last chapter, I should hope to have you write that even a scoundrel can be turned into an honest man by such a girl as Kate.'

"That's what he said. I been sayin' it over and over to myself because I might of forgot it. That was just what he said."

"It is quite enough and a great deal too much!"

"Maybe. When I told you that, I was to watch your face mighty close and then to tell him just the way you looked."

"Willie!" cried the girl.

"Sure, that was what he told me."

"But you won't do it!"

"Won't I? Miss Murran, when he ain't got no other friends, don't I have to stand by him?"

She clasped her hands. She felt herself growing younger and weaker. She felt Willie expanding in years and in size — a monster in whose mercy she was.

"What will you tell him, then?"

"Nothin' but the truth."

"The truth — the truth! What do you know about the truth?"

"Nothin' but what I seen and heard!"

"That isn't always — what will you tell him, Willie?"

"Why, only about the way that you got sort of pink."

"Willie!"

"And the way that you frowned, but got sort of crinkly around the eyes, like you

290

was lookin' at the sun."

"Willie!"

"It's the truth."

"Willie, I'll never be able to lift my head again —" She added, suddenly, with both hands pressed to her heart: "Ah, what will become of him? Wild man — wild man! Would he dare to come into San Pablo simply to tell me those things? Would he dare to do that? Oh, Willie!"

He took one of her hands in his two grimy fists. "Shall I tell him this?" asked Willie.

"What, Willie?"

"About the way you cried and took on?"

"I don't care! I don't care what you tell him!" said Kitty Murran. "But what will become of him? Who will save him, Willie?"

CHAPTER 29

At this, she became aware of a change in the boy. He drew a little back from her and regarded her with a sort of wistful sorrow, as though she were greatly changed for the nonce, in his eyes.

"I sort of thought it was this way," said Willie. "But I wasn't sure. I'm mighty sorry."

"For what? Willie, what a terrible boy you are! You have only been guessing all this while?"

"Maybe."

"Now why are you sorry? Confess that you've only been pretending to like him?"

"Him? Miss Murran, him and me are — partners!" He swelled as he spoke the words. "Partners!" repeated Willie. "But why I'm sorry — it's because I don't see how he'll get away when he shows himself at the hotel this noon."

"At the hotel! Willie —"

"He told Rankin that he'd be there!"

"You mean that he'll keep that promise?

That mad promise?"

"You couldn't noways think of him breakin' his word. He ain't that kind."

"But to come to San Pablo is wild enough. To show himself near the hotel at noon — that would be madness!"

"He ain't like other folks."

"Tell me only this. Did he tell you that he would be there to-day?"

"He don't do no braggin'. He just up and does things without talkin'. That's Corcoran."

At this, her eyes grew large and dark, then bright and small.

"Thank God, then, that there will be few people in the street at that time."

"Why?"

"Because it's the noon hour, of course, and they'll be having their lunch."

"Wouldn't they miss all their meals for three days for the sake of seein' Corcoran fight?"

"But will they expect him to do such a foolish, crazy thing as to put his head in the lion's mouth?"

"They know a lot more about Corcoran, ma'am."

"Enough to make them think —"

"That they ain't nothin' that he wouldn't try to do if he was dared!"

"Oh, God keep him from such a thing! Willie, Willie, what shall I do? Do you think that Henry Roland could help him?"

"Corcoran would choke if he thought that Roland ever done him a good turn."

"I know. I — where can I go? Who'll help him? Who'll help *me!*"

"I will," said the boy. "But dog-gone little good I can do when it comes to a gun play. Me not havin' a gun!"

"It has to be stopped!" cried she. And she fled straight-way to find the sheriff.

Mike Nolan was not in his office. Neither was he in the saddle careering across the open country on the trail of the fugitive. But, being of a philosophical turn of mind, he first alarmed the near-by towns via the telegraph. Then he went home to hoe a berry patch in his back yard. It was there that Kate Murran found him, his stubby pipe in his mouth, grunting as he worked, with his sombrero on the back of his head and the smell of newly broken loam underfoot and about him, mingled with the strong odor of his burning tobacco.

"What's the news?" said he, touching the brim of his hat to the schoolteacher. "Have the boys cornered Willie and pummeled him good, at last?"

"Oh, no."

"Has Willie knocked the stuffin' out of about a dozen of 'em, then?"

"It's not Willie," said she.

"Well?" said the sheriff, and paused.

She realized, suddenly, that her errand was most strange. In fact, there was hardly any way in which she could begin to speak.

"Because," explained the sheriff kindly, "mostly folks never come to see me except when they got trouble on hand."

"Tell me," she asked impetuously, "what manner of man is Thomas Corcoran?"

At this, the sheriff pushed back his hat, ostensibly to wipe his steaming brow, but in reality because he wished to have time to ponder this question before he answered it.

"They's two ways of lookin' at Corcoran," he said at last. "They's some that says he's a hero. They's some that says he's a cheatin' thug. Which way do you look at him, Miss Murran?"

She shook her head until her hair fluffed pleasantly beneath the brim of her hat.

"I don't know, Mr. Nolan. Which is the right way?"

"That," said the sheriff, "would take a dog-gone prophet to make out, and when he got through makin' out, most like the prophet would be all wrong."

"Ah," said the girl, "I see that you like him!"

"Do you? Then you see a lot more'n I do!"

"But is it true?"

"What?"

"That he'll come back to San Pablo to-day to meet that — that terrible Cracken at noon?"

"I dunno," said the sheriff. "Maybe he will; maybe he won't. I could say this: They ain't no other man in the world that would take a fool chance like that! No one but Corcoran. But him — he's apt to do almost anything that ain't expected."

"What do you think?"

"Me? I think that he'll come. Think of the advertisin' it would be."

"It would be certain death!"

"Wouldn't Corcoran die for the sake of advertisin' like that?"

"He can't be such a hare-brained fool!"

"Fool? Well, I dunno. Maybe he is and maybe he ain't. Speakin' personal, I'll be on deck at the hotel about noon, I figger."

At that, she saw the picture suddenly painted to the life. She heard the beat of hoofs down the dusty street. She saw the horseman swerve into view. She saw Joe Cracken stop and stiffen in his tracks. Out of the dust cloud she saw the gleam of the raised gun. Then the roar of the revolvers, the fall of Cracken, and Corcoran ride on with the great gray horse. Ride on into what? A swirl of smoke, a crackling of many guns. So, with an empty saddle, she saw the gray flee down the street. And Corcoran lay in the dust behind him!

Such was the picture from which she looked up into the kind face of Mike Nolan.

"What does it mean to you?" he was asking her.

"Nothing!" said Kitty Murran, and tried her courageous best to smile.

At this, the sheriff scowled black as night.

"He's been talkin' some to you, I guess," said Nolan. "Maybe he's got you to thinkin' that they's worse men in the world than Tom Corcoran."

"But are there not?"

"Ah," said Nolan, "that's the question. But speakin' personal, if I wished him captured before, I got to wish him dead now!"

"Sheriff —" whispered the girl tremulously.

He took her arm and led her to an old rustic chair under the grape arbor.

"Maria!" he thundered.

The wife appeared hastily on the porch above them, the screen door slamming heavily behind her.

"M'ria, get some water, quick."

"Why, Michael, what's happened? It ain't Miss Murran!"

"It's her. Don't stop to do no talkin', woman!"

The water was brought in a whirl of haste. Mrs. Nolan supported the head of the girl; the sheriff placed the glass at her lips.

"I am quite all right," whispered she, looking up, and straightway sagged in the chair again.

"Heavens above!" moaned Mrs. Nolan. "Nothin' ain't happened to Henry Roland?"

"Not him," said the sheriff tersely. "You just shut up, M'ria, and fan her with your apron."

She obeyed. The eyes fluttered open again.

"It's all right," said the sheriff.

"You won't let it happen!" moaned the girl.

"Nothin' ain't goin' to happen," said the sheriff through his teeth.

"What on earth —" began Mrs. Nolan.

"She's got touched with the sun," said the sheriff.

"Poor dear! Are you feelin' a mite better, Miss Murran?"

She sat up, trembling, staring at the sheriff. "Oh, I'm quite all right."

"You ain't, though. You come inside and I'll make you comfortable. They ain't nothin' to do except to lie down for a spell."

"Run along, M'ria," said the sheriff, "I'll take her in. Run along and fix up a bit of toddy. That'll brace her up."

Mrs. Nolan disappeared up the steps with clattering heels; the sheriff followed slowly, helping the girl strongly with his hands beneath her elbows.

"It mustn't happen!" sobbed Kate Murran. "Sheriff, he's a good man. I don't care what people say of him. I know that he's a good man. He — he —"

"Maybe he told you so," muttered the sheriff beneath his breath, but he added aloud: "Tell me one thing — is he your man, Kate?"

And she said, looking up to him through her tears: "Will you help me, no matter what the law wants you to do?"

"Law?" said the sheriff. "I don't give a darn for the law. I'm here workin' for the happiness of folks."

CHAPTER 30

When Mike Nolan started to work, he was rarely at a loss for a first effective step. He went straight to the gambling house of Theodore Rankin. Even at midday it was not entirely deserted. At all times there were a few remaining who had not lost quite all their money the evening before, and who therefore wished to try their fortune to the dregs on the following day. So they remained at the valiant task of losing money as fast as fortune, assisted by crooked card tricks, could take it from them, which was usually fast enough.

At the door of Rankin's place, the sheriff paused and said to the first man: "Get Rankin."

The other stared at him for a single frightened instant. All of the illegal devices of Rankin were not known even to the most intimate of Rankin's associates in the business, but all knew enough to understand that he was out of jail only by the good graces of luck and the law of the frontier community which is kindly and blind to sinners who do less than steal the life. However, in half a minute Theodore Rankin came hurrying out through the door of his place and greeted the sheriff with his best smile. On a time, Rankin had been a hardware salesman, and he had never forgotten the trick of smiling which he had learned as front doors were opened.

"Dog-gones if I didn't hear that you was usin' up hossflesh at the rate of three horses a day, sheriff," said Rankin as he appeared. "But maybe the hunt is done, sheriff. Otherwise, we wouldn't have you back here in San Pablo. Mighty glad to see you, Nolan."

"I know how glad you are to see me, friend," said the sheriff. "I know a pile about you, Rankin, but the time ain't come for us to talk about the way we understand each other. Right now, what I want to know about is one of your hired men."

Rankin, like an adept, put the vicious part of this remark out of his mind. "One of my men? They been cuttin' up? Name him and take him, sheriff. I won't stand in your way, none. I aim to help the law that helps me."

"Thanks," said the sheriff. "Maybe I'll be callin' you out for posse duty, one of these here days. But him that I want to know about now is this man Joe Cracken."

"Joe? Why, sheriff he's a quiet, law-abidin' gent. Joe Cracken is one of the best —"

"The devil, Rankin," said the sheriff. "I tell you I know the name he used to wear when you first met up with him. Don't try none of that talk on me. I know the name that he was wearin' when you first come up with him down in Tulsa, once."

"Why," said Rankin, blinking, but otherwise unabashed, "you're an odd sort, sheriff. You got a long eye and a long memory. Something I ain't been blessed with, dog-goned if I have!"

"Cracken," went on the sheriff, "has killed five men. And if he lives out a nacheral life, he'll kill five men more, and every one of 'em will be a better man than he is. Because, Rankin, Cracken is a skunk. But I ain't dwellin' on that, none. What I want to know is this: Is Cracken gunna step out by the hotel along about noontime of to-day, or is he gunna be takin' a siesta?"

At this, Rankin looked anxiously into the face of the sheriff. "Is there any reason why Cracken ought to be sleepin', sheriff?"

"I dunno but what there is. What's the reason that he should be there?"

"They's seven thousand five hundred good reasons. Every dollar is a reason. If

Cracken don't appear, Corcoran can get the money that Roland is holdin' for him."

"Maybe, and maybe not."

"Leastwise. *I* won't get it back, sheriff."

"What's liable to happen if Cracken goes there?"

"Sheriff, you know more about that than I do!"

"Get Cracken. I'll talk to the both of you."

So Cracken was brought and came lumbering before the sheriff with a smile on his face and both his guns limbered and loosened in their holsters.

"Where'll you be at noon?" asked the sheriff.

"In front of the hotel, if you're willin', sheriff."

"How come?"

"I give my promise to the folks that I'd be on hand."

"Cracken, if you go there, you'll be salted away with lead."

"Me?"

"Cracken, I know a pile about you, more than you think. I know about the things you done in New Mexico. I know about the things that you done in Old Mexico. I knowed about 'em long before you ever come to this here town. The kind of books that I read, they've had a mighty pile to say about you and your work. I know you're a fast man and a mighty sure man. But, Joe, you ain't fast enough and you ain't sure enough to match up with Corcoran. That's all there is to it."

Joe Cracken looked with a swift glance at his chief, but Ted Rankin, gnawing his lips, was staring from one to the other, unable to speak, unable to tell in what way he should even think.

So Cracken, left to himself, shook his head. "I got to be there," he said. He added, a little sharply: "Is they any good reason you got thinkin' that Corcoran'll be fool enough to throw himself away for the sake of showin' up himself?"

"I got reasons," said the sheriff. "And I tell you, Cracken, that if you drop it'll be your own fault. You can't mate up with Corcoran. You ought to know that. He's a fightin' man by nacher and education. He's got it in his bones. He can't be licked, man to man!"

He said this last with such a voice of ringing conviction that Joe Cracken turned a sickly yellow. But he stuck to his point.

"A gent can only die once," he said. "And if I back out of this, every Chinaman from here to Butte City'll be tryin' to make me take water."

"Rankin," said the sheriff, "will you try

your hand, persuadin' him?"

But there were seven thousand and five hundred reasons why Rankin should be dumb, and dumb he remained. So Mike Nolan was forced to wander slowly down the street, filled with a sense of shame and failure. He went home and found his wife in a state of great excitement.

"She was doin' fine and comin' around quick," said she. "She was like a wilted flower, Mike, sprinkled with water. It done my heart good to see her change and get her color back. Then come a tap at the door. I went and found that good-for-nothin' imp, young Willie Kern, standin' there. Mike, why d'you leave that little mischief-makin' rat outside of the jail?"

"Because," said the sheriff, "he's worth all the rest of the boys in this here town rolled together, dog-gone me if he ain't."

"Michael!" cried the good wife. Then she went on: "He says to me: 'I want to see Miss Murran.'

" 'You'll see nothin' but trouble here, young man,' says I. 'You just run along.'

" 'Well,' says he, 'then you can drive your own pigs out of the vegetables —'

" 'Pigs!' says I. 'Heaven help us!'

"I run down and found that there wasn't nary a pig in the patch. That young rat had made up the story. When I came back, all out of breath, the first thing that I seen was dusty marks of bare feet leadin' across my clean kitchen floor. I got hold of an old broom and went in, but he was away and gone long before. And there was Kitty Murran standin' at the front door with her eyes on fire.

" 'Sit down — lie down, honey,' says I.

" 'I have to go! I have to go!' says she, pantin'.

" 'If it's for word that young rascal has brung you,' says I, 'don't pay him no heed. He'll bring you no good luck, dearie.'

" 'Willie?' says she, tossin' up her head. 'God bless him. And thank you for all your trouble, Mrs. Nolan.'

" 'Not out into the sun ag'in —' says I.

"But there she was, gone and away, and I couldn't call her back. The devil is in that young imp, Willie. How could you say that there's anything good in him, Michael?"

"I disremember what I said," remarked the sheriff in a fit of abstraction.

He went up to his own room and office combined, where he kept his files and records, his private rogues' gallery, his specimens of handwriting, his letters and his notes — not a large bulk of matter, altogether, but enough to serve as a veritable library of useful information to the good sheriff.

And there, five minutes later, his wife found him. She had stolen after and peeked shamelessly through the keyhole. And she found him sitting in his chair busily going over a revolver. She tapped hastily at the door; presently it was opened. But the revolver was out of sight.

"Mike," said she, "they's some trouble comin'!"

"Trouble?" said he faintly.

"Oh, Michael, for Heaven's sake let the young men do the fightin'! You've done your share, dear. You've done more'n your share!"

"Hush up," said Mike Nolan. "M'ria, I hope that you ain't been peekin' at me?"

"I wouldn't see nothin' but trouble if I did peek at you," sobbed the poor wife.

He put his thick arm around her shoulders. "They ain't no call for worryin'," said he. "I dunno but what it'll all come out right. Only — the trouble is M'ria, that they's liable to be more than bones busted before this here shootin' to-day is ended."

"What more than bones?"

"Hearts, and such truck," said the sheriff. "Go — lemme be alone here, honey. I got to think."

So she went out and down the stairs, slowly, for the tears were blinding her. Some day, she told herself, her children would lack a father, and her table would be faced by an empty chair. She had no hope, really; but every day she prayed to the God of mercy that he would put off the time to a far distant year.

CHAPTER 31

Whatever were the expectations of San Pablo, they were suddenly increased about eleven o'clock in the morning, for at that time the word went suddenly and softly around the town that the sheriff himself had been authority for the assertion that, without fail, the fugitive from justice would appear at noon, according to his promise, and confront Joe Cracken and all the town and all the officers of the law in San Pablo, beginning with the sheriff.

A dozen men went to see Mike Nolan.

"What will you do," they said.

"Let 'em kill one another, maybe," said Nolan. "I dunno. Maybe not!"

Then Mike Nolan found Willie Kern pelting with stones a young squirrel which had fled up toward the top of a small sapling. Around and around the trunk dodged the active little squirrel with the stones flung by the strong arm of the boy whistling near and nearer its head. Until, just as the sheriff came up, one big pebble struck its goal and the squirrel was flung out of the tree. It whirled over and over in the air, and it would never have reached the ground unharmed, for the boy raced toward the spot where it was to fall, his face illumined with savage joy, and a stick in his hand in lieu of a club. But here the hand of the sheriff descended upon his shoulder suddenly, from behind. He writhed like a young serpent around the wrist that held it, but the sheriff's grip was adamant, and from the corner of his eye Willie had the sorrow of spirit to see the squirrel land heavily on the ground, roll over like a tiny dog, gain its feet, and run staggering toward another tree.

"It's gone!" groaned Willie Kern.

"You let folks sneak up on you like this," said the sheriff, "and the gang'll have you, one of these days."

"Aw, the devil," said Willie. "I don't pay no attention to men; I just watch the kids. You being a man, I didn't watch out for you. But the dog-gone squirrel got away on account of you. That's only the third squirrel I ever slammed with a stone!"

"That," said Nolan, "is three more'n *I* ever hit with stones. I ain't had much luck even with a rifle, among 'em!"

"Well," said Willie impatiently, "what is it, Mr. Nolan?"

"This here Corcoran —"

A change came over Willie as sudden as any change which a storm wind ever worked across the face of the sky.

"What's happened to him?" asked Willie.

"You ain't a friend of his?" asked the sheriff, grinning.

"Sure I am a friend of his. Has he got into trouble?"

"Not yet. But he's almost in it."

"What sort?"

"Look here. Willie, I'm a tolerable peaceful man. You go find your friend Corcoran and tell him that. I'm a tolerable peaceful man, and I like to oblige the ladies. But I guess that I got to do my best to nab him when he tries to show up around about noon. I ain't goin' to bother him none while he's with his lady right now —"

Willie Kern turned pale as death itself. All his self-confidence was stripped from him. He merely gasped feebly upon the sheriff.

"I dunno what you mean!" said Willie.

"Ain't Corcoran with Kate Murran right this here minute?"

"Him? I dunno! Sure he ain't."

"You didn't," went on the sheriff, advancing closer to the boy with a raised forefinger, "you didn't come to my house to tell Miss Murran that the scalawag had come askin' for her? You didn't leave my house and show her the way to Corcoran —"

"Oh, my heavens!" cried Willie, shuddering. "Have you gone and got him? You ain't arrested him? You ain't goin' to hang him, sheriff?"

Sheriff Nolan stood back with a scowl. He had learned a good deal more than he had expected — much more than he cared to hear.

"Shut up, Willie," said he in haste. "If you say much more it'll be my duty to make you show me where Corcoran is."

"I'll see you go to the devil first!" said Willie with great emotion.

"I'll start out and hunt for him, then."

Willie turned paler than ever. "Very well," said the sheriff. "You don't want me to hunt for him and you don't want to lead me to him. Maybe you'll guarantee to take a message to him?"

The boy was in a torment, and standing on one foot and then on the other, he stared helplessly at the man.

"Sheriff," he said, "tell me what you want me to do. I'll do anything."

"You've sort of took to him, ain't you?"

"Him? He's a man!" cried Willie.

"I dunno but what you're halfway right," murmured the sheriff. "Leastwise, you go and tell him that if he ain't a dog-gone fool he'll keep away from the hotel around about noon. Tell him that they've tried to get Joe Cracken to keep from showin' up, but that Joe has swore he'll be there and that they ain't no way of keepin' him back. Tell him these here things. Tell him, too, that if he shows his face, I'm gonna bust myself to get him if it's the killin' of me and half the other men in San Pablo. You hear them things, Willie?"

Willie, pale and earnest, nodded. "I hear 'em," he said. "I'll remember everything."

"Do you want Corcoran to keep alive?" cried the sheriff, putting on pressure.

"Do I?" said Willie with a faint smile.

"D'you want to keep Kitty Murran from bein' a widow?"

"Sheriff —" said the boy, and then was silent, waiting.

"Then tell Corcoran all these here things that I've told you, and tell 'em loud enough for Kitty to hear 'em. You understand?"

Willie groaned. "He'd kill me if I scared her."

"She's the only one that could put a dent in him. She'll make him come to time, maybe. Remember that. Willie. She'll be

313

the only one in the world that might make him back out of a fight!"

"I'll do it," sighed Willie, "but it's mighty hard. He'll never forgive me, I guess!"

"Nonsense," said the sheriff, though he cleared his throat guiltily, "the main thing is to keep the young fool alive for the sake of the girl. Don't forget that, Willie, my man."

He watched the boy trudge away slowly, staring gloomily down at the ground. Then he himself turned off and went down the street.

In the meantime, the rumor had turned to a certainty. All through the town of San Pablo the people were certain that the celebrated Corcoran was certain to appear according to his promise before the hotel at noon, sharp. Men were willing to bet large sums that he would not fail them. Other rumors were busy. It was said that the sheriff had concerted the most elaborate plans for the capture of the gambler.

He was hailed half a dozen times as he strolled down the street.

"What's the plan, sheriff?"

"Are you goin' to catch him in a bear trap, Mike?"

To these remarks he made no answer other than a good-natured wave of his hand. But finally a voice barked: "What's this about young Roland? Is he gonna run the party that catches Corcoran?"

The sheriff had not thought of that before. Here was a trump card, the playing of which must be done with the most infinite caution. He had not hunted for five minutes before he passed young Henry Roland on the street.

Here was a change indeed! The day before, the big youth had been the proudest and the happiest man in San Pablo, with the largest fortune and the prettiest girl to his credit. But now the sheriff saw him stalking along like one whose heart is consumed by a secret pain. He was very stiff, very erect, very pale, and he looked neither to the right nor the left. Neither did his eyes see much of what was immediately before him.

"Mr. Roland!" called the sheriff.

The tall young man walked straight past him.

"Mr. Roland."

He took the arm of the younger man.

"Well, sir?" asked the sheriff.

"What will you have with me?" asked his companion sternly.

"You act as if you'd forgotten me, Roland."

"I know you very well, sir. You are Sheriff Nolan. What will you have with me, I ask you again?"

"Why," said the sheriff, "dog-gone me if you don't act sick, young man. What's wrong with you. Eh?"

"I don't understand you," said Roland.

"I think I know," said the sheriff, standing back and surveying his companion sadly and deliberately. "It's the girl, ain't it?"

"Sir!" exclaimed Roland.

"The devil, man," said Mike Nolan. "They was three girls that turned me down flat after they got engaged to me. It was the fourth one that managed to get married to me. The rest of 'em ducked out from cover. Well, it used to make me figger that I'd never be the same man ag'in, after one of them girls had walked by me. But the devil, Roland, a gent will wake up and forget all about them things! Time is what you need!"

"I haven't the slightest idea of what you're talking," said Roland. "In the meantime, I'm very busy."

"Has one of your mines caved in, then?" said the sheriff. "Or have you got bad news out of the East?"

"Nothing whatever is wrong with me or with my affairs."

"And you ain't sick?"

"Certainly not. A little overfatigued. That is all."

"Might I ask where you're going, Roland?"

"You might ask," said Roland. "And I might tell you that I only know I'm going away. Will that do for you? I only know that I'm going away from San Pablo."

"For how long?" asked Nolan.

"Forever, if God is willing."

"Give up all your friends here in San Pablo?"

"Friends?" said the big man huskily. "Friends?" And he strode off down the street with the same stiff, proud gait.

"There," said the sheriff to himself, "goes a gent that's had his heart plumb busted. It'll take till dog-gone near spring before he gets over it."

After this, like a grim-hearted man, he filled his pipe, tamped down the tobacco, lighted it, and thought of other things. Love matters surprisingly little after a man is forty-five.

CHAPTER 32

There were two main topics of conversation when the crowd gathered. The first was: Will he really come?

The second was: If he comes, how will he do it?

The answer to the first question was simply that Corcoran would never be so unkind as to disappoint such a crowd as had gathered on this day to see him. The answers to the second question were very varied. Some said that he would simply ride a horse at full gallop down the street, taking his chance of escaping bullets by the speed of his course, and shooting down Joe Cracken as he passed. And many a man vowed that if such a dashing expedient were tried he, for one, would never raise a hand against the outlaw. But there were others who had come in answer to the spreading rumor. They were hunters, and they were after the price on a man's head. From the moment that the reward was published he had been no more than a loner wolf or a coyote to them. And their rifles would not miss. Your Eastern hunter who can stalk his game through dense timber and underbrush may be a wretched marksman on occasion. But your true Western huntsman, with his far horizons and his wary game, warned by the desert silences, must learn to shoot out the eye of the sun.

Over this crowd the sheriff cast a careful eye, scanning them up and down and down and up. But still he had hope, and hope against hope.

Then he saw Willie Kern and hailed the boy. "What's happened, Willie?" he asked.

"I dunno," said Willie, looking very sick and dull. "I said what you told me to say. He took it pretty hard. He'll never forgive me."

"He's a young fool, then," remarked the sheriff calmly. "What did *she* say?"

"What did she say? Well, sheriff, she didn't leave out nothin'. I only heard the beginnin' of it. Then I was sent away."

"Will she persuade him?" groaned the sheriff.

"How could she help it?" asked Willie. "Ain't she prettier than pretty near any other girl? Ain't she tellin' him out and out that she loves him and that she'll marry him if he quits this fightin', gamblin' business?"

"Does she say that, Willie?"

"That ain't the first half of what she says, Sheriff Nolan."

"Maybe she'll win," said the sheriff. "But if you're so dog-gone confident, what makes you so pale, Willie?"

"I ain't pale," said Willie.

"You look sick, kid."

"I got a stomach ache," said Willie faintly. "But you see, the trouble is that you never can tell about that Corcoran. He ain't like other people. He — he's a gambler, you know. Maybe he'll try this here trick just for the sake of doin' the hardest thing that anybody ever tried."

"Maybe," agreed the sheriff with a sigh. And then, lifting his eyes to a window of a house across the street, he started violently.

"Willie," he commanded, "look over yonder across the street in Mrs. McCarren's second-story window."

There stood poor Kate Murran with her head leaning weakly against the side of the frame, staring sadly down at the hotel and the veranda on which Corcoran had agreed to meet Joe Cracken on this day at noon.

"Well," said Willie, "I guess it's all done for."

"I guess it is," said the sheriff in an equally doleful voice. "He's told her that no matter what she wants or what she thinks, he's gonna go through with what he promised to do."

"That's it."

"Somehow, Willie, I think a pile more of Corcoran for actin' just that way!"

"So do I, sheriff. But look at her! Doggone me if she ain't pretty near dead for fear of it."

"Go up to her, Willie, and try to make her happier."

"Me?" said Willie. "I'm right down here, sheriff, tryin' to get mixed up when the time comes."

"They ain't goin' to be no chance," said the sheriff, shaking his head. "You couldn't help Corcoran now. You can't help a thunderbolt strike!"

With this, the sheriff went on his way. He had made not the slightest preparation to receive the gambler. While the rest of the town cudgeled his brains to discover what the sheriff had prepared for the reception of Corcoran, the sheriff himself had decided that no preparation would be the best preparation. He would wait at the scene of action to do what might suggest itself to him at the time. There would be no need to call for volunteers. Five hundred men were at hand when he wished them, and all born fighters and trained fighters.

In the meantime, he kept a lookout up and down the street like the others. For in what other way could Corcoran come? Upon either side, the houses were filled — every doorway and every window — with the spectators, with men and boys and women and even little girls staring at the spectacle. It seemed to reduce the whole situation to perfect simplicity. Here was the street — a funnel open at either end. Through either end the rider might come.

"He'll come in wearin' a disguise!" said some one near the sheriff. "He'll come in wearin' whiskers, maybe. Maybe he's standin' right around near us, now. All he'll do, when he sees this here Cracken, will be to holler out something and tear the whiskers off of his face. Then when he's dropped Cracken, he'll beat it as fast as his hoss can go."

"Is they any hoss," asked another, "that can run faster'n a bullet can be drove by powder?"

There was no answer to this.

The sun was now riding high. The shadows of fences and of posts had shrunk away to negligible aprons of black over the shining white dust of the street. The wind fell away to nothing as though crushed out by the growing heat. And all the loud voices through the town of San Pablo began to die and turn into murmurs, mutterings, whispers.

"Cracken!" said a sudden booming murmur.

He came up the street slowly, as befitted one about to step into the center of the stage. He came slowly, he came quietly. One could see by his pale face and by something about his hands and his eyes — something active and restless and determined. And when some one said, "He looks pretty cool," some one else answered dryly, "He looks like he was ready to die."

Such was the opinion of the sheriff and of all the wise men in the crowd. They knew Joe Cracken and his celebrated deeds in the past. Nothing had been so thoroughly talked about during the morning of this day, but somehow none took his chances against Corcoran very seriously.

Before the veranda of the hotel, Mr. Cracken paused and loosened his two revolvers in their holsters. It was not done ostentatiously. In fact, it seemed that Mr. Cracken was quite unaware of the existence of any one other living person in the street of San Pablo. He was too entirely occupied with his own problems.

Then he deliberately turned and scanned every face in the crowd, searching, searching. And they all knew for what. Into the mind of Cracken had passed the possibility that the gambler might appear wearing a disguise, that he might come and stand by unknown in the crowd until noon came. So the traveling, studious eyes of Cracken dwelt upon each face and went on, careful, missing nothing.

When he had finished his survey without finding anything that seriously aroused his suspicions, he went onto the veranda and took a chair and leaned back against the wall of the hotel. That was one of the line of chairs which was constantly filled in front of the old hotel every day and all day. But on this occasion the chairs were empty. Not a soul disputed the sole possession of the porch which Cracken claimed.

But from the windows and from the big doorway, dozens of heads leaned out and peered at him. He was cool. There was no doubt of that. In the first place, he had dressed carefully for the part which he must play on this day. He wore around his neck a large bandanna of yellow, heavy silk, spotted with violet blue. The tip of this great kerchief dropped past the center in his back. His shirt was a sharp lavender, and was silk also. His sombrero glistened with a load of pure golden ornaments. His trousers were of the finest make, and upon his feet were shop-made boots set off with golden spurs. Such was the brilliant and costly array of Joe Cracken when he came to the battle.

"He's come out to die. A gent might as well use up all his finery on his funeral," said Mrs. McCarren, near the ear of Kitty Murran.

And then she wondered why Kitty Murran grew so very, very pale.

Not even Mrs. McCarren dared to speak after that. Not even Mrs. McCarren's oldest and most irrepressible boy had the courage to so much as whisper. There was no voice in San Pablo. There was no eye in San Pablo which was not focused upon the front porch of the hotel where a battle, in another moment or so, was about to take place. For noon was drawing perilously near. The shadows had shrunk smaller and smaller. The wind had died away to a mere nothing — a whisper which stole voicelike through the air from time to time, hushing all who heard it. And all the people who had gathered for the spectacle did not move so much as a finger, did not so much as stir their heads. They were turned to stone with their expectation.

It was at this time, when all was prepared and when every person stood with nerves drawn taut, that there was added something which might have been invented by the brain of some cheap theatrical producer, except that this being not the stage, the effect of the reality was thrilling and heart stopping. For the clock in the lobby of the hotel began to chime forth the noon hour, and its pealing rang in a small, clear voice over the quiet street.

CHAPTER 33

It was one of those old clocks which are built like a house, a tall, narrow-faced house such as might be wedged into a little street in a Dutch town, pressed thin by its equally jammed fellows, and lifting its head toward the air and sky in a thin, pinched roof chopped with a gable. Such was the clock, and it contained, behind its face with its flanking Corinthian columns and its gold-chased glass, a huge brass pendulum which was polished every Sunday morning by Zeke, the Negro porter. That pendulum had been working in San Pablo for no less than seventy years. How long it had labored before this in a certain New England town no one could have told.

It had a bell which had once spoken in a strong and solemn voice loud enough to have filled a church even when the ladies have not left off whispering. But something had happened to that voice. It had grown old, it might be said, just as the body of the clock had grown old. It had grown decrepit, just as the body of the clock had grown worm-eaten and decrepit. It was a cracked, thin voice, in short, without any resonance, and when it began to tell the hour, there was a shiver and a burr behind its every accent, so that the proprietor of the hotel used to feel that each day would be its last.

It was not a loud voice, therefore. And that was what made its far-heard chime so remarkable and portentous on this day. For in the lobby, where its call at noon had merely served to set feet pounding toward the dining room and when a roll of rising voices had usually drowned out its calling, it now floated swiftly through a void of silence. It passed across the veranda where voices were always stirring on other days, but where there was not so much as a whisper, now. It passed across the still water of the water trough under the hitching shed and beside the hitching rack. But there was no long line of horses in waiting there now, rattling the chains of their bridles, clamping their bits, stamping, squealing in anger, whinnying in recognition, grunting as riders mounted and dismounted. There was none of this. Not a horse was in sight, for, after all, even the finest shots will sometimes make a mistake when revolvers are the chosen weapons. And horses cost money.

Past the empty hitching racks floated the chime of the bell. It crossed the street. It reached the silent crowd in doorways and windows, and housewives remembered that they had never heard the noise of that flat bell before saving in the middle of the night. They had heard it ring midnight many a time; they had never before heard it chime for noon. It brought a midnight chill, indeed, into the town which listened.

And Joe Cracken was seen to jump from his chair and fall to cursing heavily.

"Joe has put himself under the gun early in the game," said some one, and the truth of that remark was generally felt.

In the meantime, slowly — with long seconds between every stroke — the clock from the hotel beat out the twelve hammer blows of noon, and the whole town of San Pablo, perspiring, holding its breath, rolling its eyes in an effort to see all things at once, listened to the last chime die out.

Would he come? Did he dare to come? It had seemed impossible that he would fail them. Now it seemed far more impossible that he should appear unless he were indeed a madman.

But, while they scanned the street up and down, there came a little stir among the thickly packed group at the door of the hotel. They were the bolder and the younger spirits of the town — the youths who were willing to risk a chance bullet and a miserable death for the sake of having first-row seats at the tragedy. These men were packed in layer upon close layer, like proverbial sardines, when a quiet voice was heard to say behind them: "If you please, gentlemen, I'd like to pass through."

"Why, you fool!" the man who was immediately addressed. "D'you think that I'll give you room? I'll see you go to the devil first!"

"My dear sir," said the voice from the rear, "I am sorry to trouble you —" And the young hero felt himself taken suddenly by wrist and shoulder, his arm twitched into the small of the back, and himself turned halfway round.

He reached for his gun, but when he saw him who had disturbed him, he changed his mind, and with a faint exclamation he fell back out of the way.

That exclamation, no matter how light it was, was enough to disrupt the rest of the company like a bomb. It shattered their solidly compacted order and caused them to sag into the room and back to one side, for the word that they heard was a peculiarly compelling name, at that moment. At any rate, it forced them back into the lobby of the hotel, and left the newcomer standing alone in the doorway.

It was Corcoran. Of course, he would come by the most prominent and therefore the least expected way. How step onto the veranda of the hotel except through the front doors of the same hotel? Through them, in fact, stepped Corcoran, and he stood on the broad veranda looking the crowd over with the most perfect deliberation.

He was dressed with his usual care, all in a dark suit, with no extraordinary touch — saving his neatness in that rough town — other than his affectation of a high white stock of linen which was wrapped around his throat. It was fastened at the base of the throat by a pin with a sapphire head. Every one saw the blue glimmer of the jewel.

The ebony cane, also, was still in his hand, but it was in his left hand, now, and it was carried tucked high under his left arm as he stared up and down the street. Oh what a presence and what an eye was there! And as his eye passed over their faces the murmur was drawn from them in awe and in wonder: "Corcoran! Corcoran!"

Then he dropped the cane from beneath

his armpit and, resting the tips of his slender fingers upon its head, he completed his survey of the crowd, he leaned to flick a bit of dust from the knee of his trouser leg. And, finally, he turned to Joe Cracken. At that, the revolver leaped instantly into the hand of Cracken. But the slender right hand of Corcoran was raised in protest.

"My dear Mr. Cracken," he said, "we must not kill one another so informally. There must be a signal given. This must be done in form, really! I have come, in fact, to demand that seventy-five hundred dollars be paid to me, unless you can furnish me with a good reason why they should not be paid."

Cracken, swallowing hard, replaced his weapon in its leather holster. "I've just put up my best reason," said he.

"I've no objection to hearing it twice. What can serve as a signal to us? Suppose, Cracken, that you simply count to three. We'll keep our arms folded until you count to three. Will that serve you?"

It was giving Cracken every advantage. But he shuddered as he accepted the proposal. Finally, he stood up and faced Corcoran.

"One!" said Cracken.

"Very good," answered Corcoran, and

folded his arms, with the ebony hanging like a thin shadow from the fingers of his left hand.

"Two!"

A whisper had washed up and down the street. Those who did not understand what was happening were now informed. The whisper died out.

"Are you ready, Corcoran?"

"My dear Cracken, I'm ready whenever you say the word."

"Three!"

The gun of Cracken spoke first. It was remembered afterward with what convulsive speed it was jerked from the scabbard. And barely was its nose above the lip of the holster before it boomed, and the flying bullet whipped a long splinter from the surface of the porch and cast it across the knees of Corcoran.

As for Corcoran, his own action had been fast as light — fast as the trickster palms the card. But the dangling ebony cane had hampered his movement somewhat. He drew fast and fired from the hip at the conclusion of that swift movement. And Joe Cracken leaned forward into the air, grasping at its thinness as though it were a solid wall. Out of his right hand fell the Colt. With both hands he clutched at nothingness, and then he dropped upon his face, falling slowly, and collapsing at the last like a piece of limp cloth. His legs were twisted oddly under him; his hands were thrown out, palm up. He was dead before those hands had fallen into their final position.

"To the widow of Mr. Cracken," said Corcoran, "I am delighted to say that I give the entire claim to the money, the possession of which had brought about this dispute."

With that, he turned to one side and sauntered slowly through the door into the body of the hotel itself.

CHAPTER 34

He was out of sight before the pursuit started or before a gun was fired. Then, all together as though they had been waiting for his disappearance as for a signal, half a dozen rifles exploded and as many balls whirled through the thin air of the place where he had been standing just a little before. All they accomplished was to punch six round holes in the back wall of the hotel. Corcoran had jumped to the side the moment he was inside the doors again.

Then he found himself in the hands of some seven or eight young men who ran at him to take him prisoner. They had enjoyed the scene of the killing. Now they would enjoy equally the capture and the reward for capture of this man. Corcoran spoiled the face of one with the butt of his revolver. He knocked over another with a straight-driven blow of his skinny fist. Then he ducked through a window and dropped twenty feet, like a cat, to the ground at the rear of the hotel.

They hesitated to follow him. Twenty feet is easier to name than to do, and though Corcoran had landed safely, as for them — they preferred to send bullets after him instead of themselves. And bullets they sent, but just as he dodged out of sight around a corner of the building.

Three good men and true plunged around the back of the house at the same time and crashed straight at Corcoran. He dropped on his hands and knees until they had rushed past him, then he was up and away among the sheds.

The surroundings of the hotel seemed to have been designed for just such mischief as this. The rear of the building was occupied by an impossible tangle of fences and barns and outbuildings of a dozen sorts. It was a confused little empire, and through it Corcoran raced like a sprite. Enough lead to have pulverized his bones was sent whistling after him at one time or another in his wild career. But he avoided all danger and came, at last, straight to a shed where his own fine horse stood, ready saddled and bridled, dancing with anticipation at the sight of its returning master. As for the gallant gray which had carried Corcoran to safety before, it was now eating contentedly out of a manger in the same shed.

Alas, if the good people of San Pablo had only thought of looking somewhere, on this day, except straight at the veranda in the front of the hotel! How much they might have seen that would have benefitted them all!

Five steps away lay freedom for Corcoran. He could leap into the saddle on the beautiful black horse. God had not put in San Pablo an animal which could match its speed. And one word would send the fine creature flashing away around the corner of the first shed, and then swerving off among straw stacks until it reached the rear streets of the town, and so away into the open country. They would be very lucky if they could get within pistol shot of him or even a comfortable rifle shot by the time he was off into the open regions of the mountains.

But just as safety came into his reach, fate struck him down. Fate comes sometimes in grave and sometimes in gay apparel. But fate for Thomas Corcoran took the form of a startled pig which, a moment before, had been nipped in the rear by a darting forty-five-caliber bullet. It had barely razed the skin and brought the blood, but it stung that surprised porker like the poisoned lance of a huge hornet. So it forgot even to squeal, and with its mouth still full of parsnip root it darted around the side of the shed and fairly between the legs of Corcoran. He saw the flying danger only as a dirty gray streak before it struck him and dumped him unceremoniously on his back. His head struck a clod of plowed ground, baked hard as a rock by the sun of the mountain desert, and Corcoran closed his eyes.

It was only for an instant. He opened them again and sat up in time to be received by a dozen pairs of hands. They trussed his body so that it could not move, could hardly breathe. They then sat back and allowed the sheriff to take possession.

All that Mike Nolan said was: "Somebody put his hat on his head again. D'you want to blind the poor boy?"

Then he ordered them to raise the prisoner and carry him into the hotel. He was placed in a big chair in the lobby, where the sheriff cut away the ropes and substituted no more than a pair of handcuffs, together with loose shackles around the feet of the gambler.

Corcoran did not answer a question during all this time. He remained with a blank face until the sheriff said: "How come you to be so slow on that draw, Corcoran?"

Corcoran smiled at the sheriff. "Give me back my cane," said he, "and I'll tell you."

The sheriff complied hastily, and then waited.

"It was because Sheriff Mike Nolan was watching me," said Corcoran. "It made me nervous, you know."

That was the only satisfaction he would give. As for the rest, they made no more difference to him than if they had been wooden images. To the sheriff, however, he kept a smile and a word whenever it was wanted.

"You might think that you was his friend!" exclaimed one to Nolan.

"Well," said the sheriff, "ain't I?"

"Well, when you gonna have him tried and hung?"

"For what?"

"Why, tryin' to murder Roland; and then killin' Cracken."

"Would you have him hung for killin' Cracken?"

"That ain't what I asked you."

"Wasn't it a square fight?"

"Why —"

"Ain't Cracken had a killin' comin' to him for a long many years?"

"Look here, sheriff —"

"If they can prove that he tried to kill Roland the way that Dorn swears, he'll be sent to the jug. If they can't prove it, he'll be a free man. That's the way the thing stands."

This was in effect, but somewhat in greater detail, what he told Willie Kern.

"How can we help him?" asked Willie sadly.

"Darn it!" thundered the sheriff. "It ain't my worry, is it, what you do for him?"

"It's gunna to be the killin' of Miss Murran," said the boy gravely.

"Is she cryin' a lot?" asked the sheriff nervously.

"She ain't doin' nothin' but lyin' in the dark."

"Not makin' no noise?"

"Not makin' no sound, sheriff."

"My heavens," said the sheriff, "what a dog-gone fool a fool gambler is! Look what he's throwed away!"

So Willie retreated into the night and sat down just outside the room of Miss Murran, in the dark of the evening, thinking, listening, feeling that he would choke if he did not hear some noise of her grief, for the silence was deadly.

CHAPTER 35

Take it all in all, it was a capture out of which the town of San Pablo received far less enjoyment than it had anticipated. The fight had been all that it could have wished. And San Pablo felt somewhat like part of an audience at a prize fight which, having been well entertained, nevertheless abuses the combatants.

One man lay dead for the amusement of San Pablo. Another man was in jail. But perhaps in all of the town there was only one person who rejoiced heartily. That was the same Gabriel Dorn whose inventive tongue, in the first place, had brought the main trouble upon the head of Corcoran.

It meant for him perfect security. Having bearded the lion, he now beheld the paws of the lion chopped off by the ax of the law. What could have been more delightful for Gabriel Dorn?

On this night, therefore, he began taking his whiskey before supper, and continued until well after that meal. Liquor did not often confuse his brain. It merely enfeebled his body, and when a knock came at the door, he leaned heavily in the opening.

It was Willie Kern who stood before him.

"Miss Murran, she wants you quick, Mr. Dorn," said the boy seriously.

"She wants me, does she?" sneered Gabriel. "I thought that she was too wrapped up in —"

"Gabriel!" cried the sharp voice of his mother from the rear of the room.

"All right!" muttered Gabriel Dorn. "What does she want of me?"

"I dunno," said Willie. "She says that you're the only man who can help her."

"Of course," said Gabriel. "If that's the case, I'll be along at once." He huddled himself into a hat and coat.

"Gabriel, you are mad!" exclaimed his mother. "You're more than half drunk, and she'll know it."

"I'm more than half drunk," declared the amiable Gabriel, "but Kitty's a fool. She'll never know it. What the devil could she need of me?"

"Wait for half an hour — soak your head in some cold water, Gabriel, dear —"

"Shut up!" said Gabriel dear, and reeled away through the open door into the night, and left that door open behind him, so that the feeble light from the lamp went flickering out into the night.

"Want me to steady you?" asked Willie.

"No, darn you, keep out from between my feet — or I — Which way are you trying to take me?"

"She's over to Mrs. McCarren's aunt's place."

Gabriel Dorn, still upon unsteady legs, crossed the road and entered the thicket on the farther side.

"Hey!" he called suddenly. "This isn't the way —"

He turned toward his guide, only to find a sinewy leg inserted suddenly between his, and he was pitched heavily upon his back, where Willie Kern jumped on his chest and rode him with a sharp-pointed knife at the base of Mr. Dorn's throat. Gabriel drew in his breath to shriek for help. A deeper prick of the knife silenced him.

"I'll cut your head off!" snarled out Willie Kern.

"You'll hang for this, boy!" cried the coward. "You'll —"

"That there lie you told about Corcoran —" said Willie Kern. "About him hirin' you to kill Roland — will you write out this it *was* a lie?"

343

"Who got you to do this?" snarled out Dorn.

"Will you write it out?" asked Willie remorselessly.

"Take that knife away. Take it away before you cut my throat — by mistake. I'll — I'll write anything!"

It was a very odd scene. Gabriel Dorn sat crosslegged with an old envelope upon his knee. With one hand he lighted matches; with the other he wrote, and behind him leaned Willie Kern, reading the writing and keeping the sharp needle point of the knife in the small of Mr. Dorn's back.

The first statement was briefly scribbled down. But when Dorn was about to sign his name, Willie checked him.

"Where'd you get that hundred dollars that they found on you?" he asked.

"I'll see you damned before I tell that!" gasped out Mr. Dorn.

"Write 'er down!" growled Willie, and Mr. Dorn, feeling the horrible point of the knife glide deeper into his flesh, wrote:

"Ted Rankin gave me the hundred as part payment if I'd kill Corcoran."

Then he signed, and the paper was snatched from his hand. When he rose, Willie had darted away into the night. And Mr. Dorn, realizing that mounted men would be hunting for him within some ten minutes, fled madly through the night.

What became of him no one was ever able to tell. He faded from San Pablo and was never seen again. Some said that he must have raced the entire distance across country until he came to the railroad, and that he then must have ridden the brake beams to the far East. At any rate, he was gone out of the lives of Corcoran and Kate Murran.

As for Corcoran, it was freely admitted that he had killed Cracken in open fight. Nothing could have been fairer. The stealing of the gray horse amounted to nothing. Had not the animal been returned sound? And as for the statement of Mr. Dorn, there was the recantation of that worthy gentleman!

So, before San Pablo had time to more than draw its breath, Mr. Corcoran was liberated from the jail.

He found in the sheriff's office, the sheriff himself, Kate Murran, and Henry Roland. Mike Nolan became the spokesman.

"Corcoran," he said, "we been talkin' over your affairs. And the long of it is that, seein' that you and Miss Murran aim to agree together — for life — Mr. Roland here says that he has got to do something to square things with you. He says that you got a debt against him. Is that right?"

The hand of Corcoran raised slowly to his face and his finger tips touched a small bruised place on his jaw.

"Oh," said he, "as for that, I have quite forgotten it, if Mr. Roland is willing to forget."

Mr. Roland swallowed.

"I shall forget nothing," he said huskily. "But, having acted like a hound through a large part of this affair, I at least would like to shake your hand, Corcoran, and wish you and Kate eternal happiness."

"I am a thousand times obliged, Roland," said the former gambler. "There is only one matter that you mistake. The name is Burlington, Roland. Corcoran, you know, is dead, and lies buried somewhere in San Pablo."

The employees of Thorndike Press hope you have enjoyed this Large Print book. All our Thorndike and Wheeler Large Print titles are designed for easy reading, and all our books are made to last. Other Thorndike Press Large Print books are available at your library, through selected bookstores, or directly from us.

For information about titles, please call:

(800) 223-1244

or visit our Web site at:

www.gale.com/thorndike
www.gale.com/wheeler

To share your comments, please write:

Publisher
Thorndike Press
295 Kennedy Memorial Drive
Waterville, ME   04901